Also by Brian Doyle

Boy O'Boy
Mary Ann Alice
The Low Life
Uncle Ronald
Spud Sweetgrass
Covered Bridge
Easy Avenue
Angel Square
Up to Low
You Can Pick Me Up at Peggy's Cove
Hey, Dad!

Spud in Winter

Spud in Winter

BRIAN DOYLE

GROUNDWOOD BOOKS
HOUSE OF ANANSI PRESS
TORONTO BERKELEY

Groundwood Books / House of Anansi Press
110 Spadina Avenue, Suite 801, Toronto, Ontario M5V 2K4
Distributed in the USA by Publishers Group West
1700 Fourth Street, Berkeley, CA 94710

We acknowledge for their financial support of our publishing program
the Canada Council for the Arts, the Government of Canada through
the Book Publishing Industry Development Program (BPIDP)
and the Ontario Arts Council.

ONTARIO ARTS COUNCIL
CONSEIL DES ARTS DE L'ONTARIO

Library and Archives Canada Cataloging in Publication
Doyle, Brian
Spud in winter
ISBN-13: 978-0-88899-755-5 – ISBN-10: 0-88899-755-8
I. Title.
PS8557.087S58 2006   jC813'.54   C2006-902347-6

Printed and bound in Canada

Thanks to Ian McKercher who introduced us to
Mongolian Fire Pot fun.
Thanks to Mike Paradis for giving me B. Faroni.
Thanks to the Glebe Collegiate E.S.L. students for
allowing me to borrow their beautiful names.
Thanks to Ryan Doyle for filling me in on CISTI.
And thanks to Jenny Doyle, my funny sister-in-law,
for giving me the school memory sequence.

Let this book be dedicated to our second grandchild who, at this writing, waits in the wings to make an entrance and be named.

I

....

I can replay it all any time I want to. Or even when I don't want to. My brain channel just goes on and plays it over. Sometimes it comes on a whole stack of screens, large and small screens, a whole wall of screens. I look away from it but then, I can't help it. I have to look back. It's hard to look away. It's like being in a big TV warehouse sale, looking at a wall of TVs, all playing the same channel. Your eyes jump from screen to screen. You try to get away. It's hard. You have to look!

The man comes out of Rocco's Cafe on the corner of Anderson and Rochester Streets, across the corner from where I live. He comes down the three snow-packed stairs and walks up Anderson Street on the north side, walking slow, lots of time. Only a few steps.

Each step crunch-squeaks on the tight snow.

He walks past a brown van with no side windows. After he's past the van he turns left into the small parking lot behind the cafe and heads towards his car.

He flicks his cigarette into the snowbank and fishes in his pocket and takes out his remote. He's fitting the remote in his hand. Now he's pointing the remote at his fancy car, getting ready to unlock his fancy door. Now he's taking the second-last step he'll ever take in his life.

He's dressed in a pair of perfect, pressed, light-blue pants, shiny gray boots with high heels, a black belt with a fancy leather buckle, a bright-pink long-sleeved shirt unbuttoned down the front. He has no undershirt on. He has a big silver watch, diamond-shaped cufflinks, different-colored rings on his fingers and a gold chain around his neck that hangs down in the hair on his chest, and one small earring. His hair is curly and tight to his head.

He's carrying his overcoat. It's a record-cold day and he has this beautiful fur coat. But he's not wearing it, he's carrying it.

He's carrying it because he'll soon be in his car and it's warm in there because he's left it running and it's all heated up just waiting for him.

He's just had a nice hot cup of espresso coffee at Rocco's Cafe, put his beautiful fur coat over his arm, waved goodbye to his friends there and walked out to get into his heated car.

His breath curls around his head like steamy perfume.

Out of a small square hole in the end of the van comes a narrow pipe.

The pipe jumps and there's a crack, then a boom and then an echo off the houses on Rochester and Anderson Streets, the corner where I live.

The man, who just had the nice hot cup of coffee, dives head first into the side of his car and then bounces off the frozen parking lot. His arms and legs and his head don't seem to be his own anymore. He flops down there like a doll made of cloth.

The man in the pink shirt is now down on the snow beside his fancy car. The burglar alarm in his car is yipping away as the echo of the rifle fades.

The man's fur coat is partly over his legs, and there's blood growing in the snow.

It's playing on all my TV screens at once. The screens of my mind. I have to look.

The pipe disappears into the square hole in the rear of the van.

The van begins to move slow away from the curb.

It's cold. It's minus 31 degrees and sinking.

The tires creak and crack on the frozen solid snow of the street. The sun is bright but there's nothing warm about it. The exhaust from the van piles up behind it like steam from a chipwagon. The windows are tinted. You can't see the driver.

The van is a ghost.

But wait!

The driver is leaning close to the window to check his mirror as he begins to pull away from the curb. And now. Yes.

Now I see him.

Just for a second. No, not a second. Not that much. Less than that. Just a glimpse.

Just a flash.

But it's not enough. Or, no! Maybe it's too much!

My memory is a stop-action. A freeze.

The driver's face, close to the tinted window for just a flash.

I see him now. I might as well have his picture in my wallet. Or in a locket around my neck. I might as well have his picture in a frame on my bureau in my bedroom.

His face is square and strong. His jaw is dark, almost blue where he shaves. His eyes are wide apart. His lips are carved, like out of wood, and his little mustache is neat and could be drawn there with a pencil. His eyebrows are thick and almost meet each other over his nose. His forehead juts out over his small black eyes. His hair is big and black and perfect. You can tell he takes very good care of his hair. You can tell he loves his hair. That he looks in the mirror at his hair every chance he gets.

The muscles in his jaw are clenched, making his face hard.

He looks right at me but I don't know if he sees me or not. I'm leaning up against the old brown doors that lead into my backyard. The doors and my coat are the same color.

Can you look right into a person's face without seeing that person?

I hope so.

I hope so because I know this guy.

He's a regular customer of my friend, Connie Pan.

Connie Pan does this guy's hair all the time at the Hong Kong Beauty Salon where she works!

She's often told me about him, and we laughed about how much this guy was so madly in love with his own hair! This is the guy!

And, one day, when I went into the Hong Kong Beauty Salon, she secretly pointed to him as he was looking in the mirror. He was putting on his scarf. You don't need to look in a mirror to put on your scarf. But he was looking in the mirror, watching his hair as he put on his scarf. His freshly done hair. Loving his hair!

Did he see us, in the mirror, watching him watching his hair?

This guy, who helps murder people, has had the beautiful, delicate hands of Connie Pan in his hair!

II

Call me Spud.

My real name is John. John Sweetgrass. But everybody calls me Spud. Except my mom. She calls me Johnnie.

I first got called Spud when I got a job in a chipwagon. Working with potatoes.

That was only last summer. It seems so long ago now. But it's really only a few months ago that I met Connie Pan and then got kicked out of school (not because of Connie Pan!) — Ottawa Technical High School on Albert Street — and when I got my picture in the paper and when they said, under the picture, that I was a hero.

A hero for helping to catch a polluter named Angelo "Dumper" Stubbs.

My friend Dink the Thinker helped me to catch Dumper, but Dink didn't get his picture in the paper.

My guidance teacher says that one of the reasons I got back in school was that getting my picture in the paper was good for my "self-esteem." I told my guidance teacher, The Cyclops, that I felt bad that Dink didn't get praised up, too, for what he did, how he helped me.

"That doesn't matter," says The Cyclops (everybody calls him that because he only has one eye). "Your friend Dink doesn't need any more self-esteem." Then The Cyclops looks right at me with his one eye. "He already has enough self-esteem," says The Cyclops.

How can you have too much self-esteem? Guidance teachers. How do they know if you have enough self-esteem or not? Do they have a self-esteem meter wired into your chair that registers your self-esteem while you sit there, getting guided?

Anyway, they sent the slob, Dumper Stubbs, off to jail and I'm back in school with Dink the Thinker and Connie Pan and it's pretty good. Mostly it's pretty good because the teacher who got me hoofed out in the first place isn't here anymore. Mr. Boyle, hot shot, is gone.

He's probably half drunk somewhere, sitting in some strip joint watching the women take their clothes off while they're standing on his table. Well, he can't do that at Valentino's on Somerset Street anymore because Valentino's burned down a little while ago. Dink and I caught him coming out of there one time.

I guess things just got too hot in there.

Self-esteem.

I used to think self-esteem was when you got all steamed up about yourself. All puffed up because you were full of hot air.

My father once told me he knew an old Abo chief who was so full of self-esteem that he put on his huge, fancy, full headdress of beautiful feathers one day and got so proud of himself that he blew up.

My father said there were feathers coming down out of the sky like snowflakes for days and days after. A blizzard of feathers. A self-esteem storm.

My father was a funny man.

He was an Abo.

An Ojibway type Abo.

He's dead now.

I loved him.

He died of a brain tumor.

I told my guidance teacher about the old Abo chief who exploded.

The Cyclops didn't laugh or smile or anything. People who don't laugh shouldn't be allowed to be teachers.

I'll probably go back to the chipwagon business next summer. Mr. Fryday, the Classical Chip Man, doesn't need as many people to work for him in the winter, so he laid me off.

But we're still friends.

I see him, now and again, making his rounds to some of the chipwagons he owns, all named after classical music composers.

My wagon was called Beethoven's Chips. Maybe you've heard of it.

Mr. Fryday is very good for my self-esteem. He's always praising me up every time he sees me.

He always says something like "Spud Sweetgrass! Always a pleasure to meet again with an industrious and bright representative of the younger generation such as yourself!"

And if we're near one of his wagons, which is mostly where I run into him, he'll say, "Have an order of Mr. Fryday's Classical Fries, Spud Sweetgrass my boy! On the house!"

And then I always say, "You mean, on the *wagon*, Mr. Fryday!"

And he always laughs and lets his gold tooth twinkle.

"On the wagon! Of course! What a delightfully bright young man you are!" We always do this. In fact, I'm getting kind of sick of it to tell you the truth.

And then I always notice that he hasn't changed that dumb sign in the window of his chipwagon. The same sign he has in all of his wagons. "Come in, we're open!" says the sign. This sign is foolish. What it says. You don't go in a chipwagon. You stay outside the chipwagon. You stand outside on the sidewalk.

But I don't bother mentioning it. It isn't worth it. I tried to get him to change those signs in his wagons when I worked for him, but he just didn't seem to get it.

But, as my father would have said, his heart is in the right place.

You could drive yourself crazy thinking about these sayings.

What does that really mean, anyway, "Your heart is in the right place"?

What happens if it's in the wrong place?

What my guidance teacher, The Cyclops, doesn't know is that I have enough self-esteem. I've had it since that night when I was nine.

When my parents left me alone all night on the shore of One Man Lake, with only a knife, a fishing line and one wooden match. And in the morning, when they returned, I was sitting by my fire cooking a fish for breakfast. Victorious! I survived!

My mom likes to go over to the Village Inn across the street after work to have a rye and ginger ale and talk with her friends at the table where they all used to sit when my father was alive.

She always sits in the same place.

Beside the empty chair. My father's chair.

Where he always sat.

Nobody ever takes that chair when my mom and her friends are there. Now and then, maybe a stranger might try to sit in it or ask to borrow it but somebody always politely says no and explains it all.

Explains how my father, the Abo who played the trombone, was so loved by everybody and is so missed by everybody.

There's only one person allowed in that chair. That's me, John Spud Sweetgrass.

When I go over to the Village Inn sometimes to see my mom, I sit in the special chair beside her and it feels good. I like the way the others look at me and talk to me. I feel special.

Self-esteem.

III

It's all in the paper. The *Ottawa Citizen*. A known criminal named Al Laromano is shot in the parking lot of Rocco's Cafe on the corner of Anderson and Rochester Streets in Centertown, Ottawa.

Right where I live.

Don't get me wrong. Living around where I live isn't dangerous.

Nobody is afraid to go out at night alone around my place. You can go out all by yourself and nobody will attack you or mug you.

It's the safest place in Ottawa around where I live.

A girl could go out at night all by herself for a walk or to the store and she wouldn't be scared.

Grampas or grannies aren't afraid to sleep out on the veranda by themselves on the hot summer nights.

A kid can go down to the park and the parents don't have to worry.

It's a safe place to live.

Except for the criminals.

If you're a criminal, you have to be careful. You might be wiped out by the other criminals.

Around my place, the criminals are always trying to get rid of the other criminals.

And they often seem to have funny names when one of them disappears or gets killed and you read about it in the paper.

Once my friend Dink the Thinker saw in the *Ottawa Citizen* the name of a guy who was killed after he stole a whole pile of money from a road construction company. His name was Hammer. Jack Hammer.

Dink started making up names that would be good for different criminals. The first one he made up was the name of the head of a gang of cigarette smugglers. Nick.

Nick O'Teen.

And the museum thief, Art Gallery. And Vic Tim, the hit man. And Mort Tuary, the body parts salesman. And the car cannibal, Axel Grease? And the guy who hijacked the huge Head and Shoulders transport truck? His name? Dan, of course. Dan Druff.

And Stu, the bank robber who locked himself in the vault by mistake? His last name? You guessed already! Pidity!

But back to Al Laromano.

The paper says it's part of a crooks' war and that Laromano is a suspect in another murder where two guys were gunned down in a cafe on Booth Street.

Right near my place.

The paper also says that Laromano was associated in some way with another guy, Paddy O'Doors, who was found sticking out of a sewer near a cafe on Eccles Street.

The street Dink lives on.

Then another guy who was running away from two other guys last summer tried to go through a plate-glass window like they do in the movies and got cut up into many slices, like a big salami.

That happened on Cambridge Street, the street of Connie Pan.

Then the paper says the police won't say if there's a witness to this latest shooting or not. The police won't tell if anybody came forward and told them that they saw something.

Then the paper says that the police think if there was a vehicle involved then there was probably more than one person who committed this crime. The crime of murder.

All day in school today I'm going around in a dream. Everybody's asking me what it's like to live on a street where murder is committed right outside your bedroom window.

The scene yesterday is rolling and replaying again and again on the screen of my mind.

It's like seeing the same part over and over again from a movie they're advertising on the Movie Channel. You get so used to it you know it off by heart. And you get to hate it.

You want to switch it off.

I'm in French class, trying to change the channel in my head.

I'm watching our French teacher, Mademoiselle Tarte au Sucre, trying to teach us French.

None of the guys in the class can learn any French from Mademoiselle Tarte au Sucre because of the way she looks. She wears long dresses that are so tight that when she walks she has to take tiny steps. It takes about twenty steps for her to get from her desk to the blackboard.

And she wears high heels so high that she's almost on tiptoes as she tries to get to the blackboard. When she finally gets there, all the guys in the class have completely forgotten about what she just tried to teach us in French.

She has about ten different types of bracelets on her left arm, the arm she writes on the blackboard with. While she's writing, she uses her right hand to push her long golden hair back over her shoulder while the bracelets on her left arm play sort of a little French song.

All this makes the guys want to jump up and start dancing or rapping. It doesn't make them want to learn French, though.

Mademoiselle Tarte au Sucre wears so much perfume that you can start to smell her out in the hall even before she gets in the room.

Her fingernails are painted with stuff that glows in the dark. On some days she has a pretty little stencil of a bug of some kind on each nail. A butterfly, a grasshopper, a ladybug, maybe. It must take hours to put all this stuff on.

Dink the Thinker once said he estimated that she would have to get up at four o'clock in the morning to have enough time to get herself ready to come to work.

She wears a silver bracelet around her ankle and a locket on a chain around her throat, shaped like a heart.

A lot of the guys say that inside the locket she has a picture of The Cyclops.

I don't know why, but I always burst out laughing

every time I hear that. I see, in my mind, The Cyclops with his one eye, leaning close, studying the little bugs on Tarte au Sucre's fingernails.

Now I'm replaying yesterday again. I can't help it.

It's minus 32 degrees now. A record for this day in Ottawa.

The dead crook in the parking lot doesn't mind the cold.

And the big crowd that's growing there, they're ready to put up with anything to get a look at the dead body. They want to see the cops, feel the excitement.

Mothers with their kids and grampas and grannies of all shapes and sizes and colors have come to see. People have poured out of the Village Inn to have a look. People hanging out of upstairs windows, standing in doorways hugging themselves, going back for coats, crowding on the verandas and in the laneways.

Cars double-parked all over the place and lights flashing and sirens bleeping and crying. People shouting and laughing and giving orders.

The police want to know who phoned them.

"Is the individual present who first notified police via 911 regarding this incident?" a big fat policeman is shouting into a horn.

"Would the responsible citizen be kind enough to

come forward and identify himself? We'd appreciate your cooperation. Thank you!"

The fog coming from the cars and the open doors and windows of the houses and the breaths of the crowd is getting so thick that the star of the show is starting to disappear. The main attraction. You can hardly see the blood in the snow and the pink shirt and the fur coat over the legs.

People are talking and giggling and stomping their feet and banging their mitts together. It's like a party.

There's a little kid propped up in a snowbank. He's so wrapped up he doesn't look human. There's another kid in a wooden box which is nailed to a toboggan. He's got so many clothes on he can't move his arms or turn his head. His mother, who is pulling the toboggan, has hardly any clothes on at all. A little short skirt, tiny high-heeled boots, a short little coat, a hat about the size of a snowball. Earmuffs the shape of baby rabbits. Her throat is bare. It shows a big gold necklace.

Somebody says the temperature is now down to minus 33 degrees. Another record for this day. People argue. How can you have two records set in one day? There's only one record-cold temperature!

My friend Dink the Thinker would now tell you the estimated temperature of the gold necklace around the mother's throat. He knows stuff like that.

Over there is a bag lady with two shopping carts tied together with a chain. The carts are tied side by side and she's stuck in the snow. Back and forward, back and forward cursing, stuck, the wheels stuck in the snow. Both carts are packed full. She can't get one more thing in there. But what is all that stuff? Can anybody tell what she's got in there? What she's collecting?

Why am I noticing all these things? Maybe it's because I'm avoiding thinking what I should be thinking of. "Avoiding the issue," my mom calls it.

Here come a couple of kids dressed up in the latest style. The latest style is easy to figure out. Just make sure everything you wear is ten times too big for you.

And make sure that from the back, the ass of your pants looks like you just dumped a big load in there. There's enough cloth in the pants on these two geeks to keep all the bag ladies in the city of Ottawa warm all winter long.

And then to be right in style make sure your hat is too small for you. It helps if your head is pointed. These kids are right in style. One of them has a head so pointed he could wear a thimble for a hat. The other one has a head shaped like a banana.

Why am I thinking about these things? To avoid thinking about what I have to think about, that's why.

There's a jogger coming through the huge crowd. There's stuff hanging from his mustache. It's ice. Icicles are also growing out of his nose. As he comes through the crowd, he says excuse me, excuse me.

Even a murder won't stop a jogger. If a guy was lying dead on the road, a jogger would probably step right over him and keep going.

There's a Vietnamese kid letting some other kids in his back door so they can go up on the wooden balcony where his mother has her clothesline. They can watch the show from there. The kid is charging admission. A bite of your chocolate bar. A quarter. A hockey card.

Over here, two dogs are fighting while another one watches.

And friends of the shot crook are standing around the cafe.

Shocked. They were just talking to him a few minutes ago, weren't they? How could you be dead if you were alive just a few minutes ago?

I notice all these things to keep one thing out of my mind.

Should I talk to the police?

Will I be in danger?

Can a person look at you without seeing you?

Will Connie Pan be in danger?

Did the driver of the brown van see, that day he was looking in the mirror in the beauty salon, putting on his scarf, admiring his hair, did he see that Connie Pan, his hairdresser, was a friend of mine? Did he see me?

Now, who's this coming through the crowd?

A woman in a kind of ski outfit with a black book in her mitt. She's talking to people as she moves in and out of the crowd. She's very close now. I can hear what she's saying. She's showing people her badge in the black book and saying who she is and asking if anybody knows who phoned in the call to report the shooting. She's also asking did anybody see anything, notice anything, hear anything?

Her name is Detective Sergeant Marilyn Kennedy. She's taller than my mom and about as tall as I am. She has a beautiful soft face and huge blue eyes. She's quiet-spoken and patient. But she seems strong at the same time. People pay attention when she speaks.

She's right next to me now.

I'm looking in her eyes and I can't look away when she asks the question. I want to look away but I can't.

"I did," I say quietly. "I called it in."

Detective Kennedy leans her head in closer. I know she heard me but she wants me to talk even more quiet than quiet. Sometimes when people lean their head in, it's because they want you to talk louder. But sometimes it's the opposite. This is the opposite.

"I called it in," I whisper. "I saw somebody."

For a second, the smoke of our breaths makes one cloud. One cloud and we are in it, face to face.

IV

Sometimes Dink's dad acts like he's going to choke to death. Dink's dad is a cigarette junkie and when he gets a real good coughing fit going, I can't help getting worried. Dink's dad's cough has three parts. The beginning of Dink's dad's cough is like a rifle shot. The middle part lasts so long that his face goes black and his eyes pour tears and his mouth stays wide open like a fish drowning in air. Then he doubles his body up and goes into the last part. It sounds a bit like somebody plunging a plugged toilet. All this time, he's not breathing and you can't help but get worried.

The three of us are watching a tape over at Dink's. The tape is an episode of "The Day the Universe Changed" that Dink taped from the Learning

Channel. It's pretty interesting the way the guy shows you how building the pyramids in Ancient Egypt was the start of us flying to Mars and living in outer space.

Of course, Dink knows the whole thing off by heart. He's seen it about fifty times. He has the whole series on tape.

I'm trying my best to listen to it but Dink's dad is sitting with us and his coughing fits don't make it any easier to hear the TV. I've got one eye on the TV and the other on him, if that's possible.

He's got his cigarette in between his first and second fingers. These two fingers are black. The rest of his smoking hand is brown.

His ashtray in front of him on the coffee table is full to the brim with butts. In fact, every ashtray in the house is full, overflowing.

Dink's dad often has two cigarettes going at once. One in an ashtray, one in his fingers or in his mouth.

All the tables in the house have cigarette burns in them.

Also, on most of the tables in the house are bottles of health pills, vitamins and iron and stuff.

You see, Dink's dad is a health nut!

In the middle of a really heavy coughing fit, he's liable to say, "Never smoke, boys! Even though the price has gone down! It's a filthy habit and it'll kill ya!"

Then he'll finish coughing, winding up staring at the floor as if he is checking to see if anything came up, like his heart, for instance!

Then he lights up another one and takes a big drag, sucking it in to get it right down as deep as he can into his body.

All around the house, Dink has put up a lot of anti-smoking posters, trying to get his dad to quit. Signs that say stuff like "It'll kill ya!" and "Don't be an idiot!" and "It will suck the life right out of you!" and pictures of half-dead-looking people who smoked for years and posters showing how much money it costs to smoke and a picture of a burnt-out lung they took out of a dead smoker and put on a table. It looks like an old shoe that was in a fire. Beside it is a picture of a nice pink lung.

I'm wondering where they got the nice pink lung. I guess from somebody who died of something else for a change.

Another poster is a picture of a revolver with the chamber open. Instead of bullets in the chamber, it's cigarettes. There's smoke coming out of the barrel.

The picture of the gun switches me to yesterday. Another channel.

Yesterday is back in front of me.

Especially the long look Detective Kennedy gives me when I say the four words, "I called it in."

Who was it called this crime in?

"I called it in." Then, "I saw somebody."

Sometimes a few easy small words, words that everybody can understand, even a little kid, can change everything.

Last spring it was only two words, two simple words I said to a teacher, that got me kicked out of school and changed my life around forever.

Detective Kennedy looks at me for a long time inside our little cloud of breath-steam. Then her eyes dart one way, then the other way. She sees that nobody around has heard me say anything. She begins to move on to the next group of people in the crowd. She begins talking to them but she keeps her eyes on me. She puts her mitt out towards me, like she's saying, Wait right there, son, don't move, don't say a word. Now she's talking to two of the waiters from the Village Inn and the cook. Now her eyes move off me but her hand is still out towards me, holding me, telling me secretly that we're together.

Now farther away.

Now I can't see her.

Then, her face again, eyes on me, telling me something. Her face now is blocked out by somebody's parka. Now her face is back, her eyes laser me through the crowd and she disappears again.

I don't move.

Now I see her head looking over a police car, her head saying, Come here or Follow me by just tilting a bit. Come here, but don't let anybody know, don't show anybody, don't reveal…she ducks in the car.

Soon the police car begins to move, slow through the frozen air and mist, and turns the corner onto Booth Street.

I walk easy, not going anywhere special, not being noticed, just strolling along away from a murder scene. If it wasn't so cold, I'd whistle a little tune. I'd whistle my father's song, "Hanging Gardens," that he composed, that he played so beautiful on his trombone.

I walk past the laneway man shoveling his laneway, even though it's already been shoveled. He doesn't look up.

He never looks up. He shovels his laneway right to the pavement. There's never a flake in his laneway. He cuts the edges of the snowbank so even and square they look like they're cut out of white marble. He cuts the snowbank along the curb like he was a surveyor or an architect. He has five or six different-sized shovels and scoops. If anybody walks up his laneway and leaves snow prints, he's right behind them with his broom and a dustpan to keep his laneway perfect. Sometimes, on a very mild day, a day when the snow will melt almost right after it hits the ground, the laneway man will shovel it first. Get it quick, before it melts! The laneway man waits in his laneway, leaning on his shovel. If a flake falls, he follows it, picking it out of the air if he can.

When the plow comes by, the laneway man is ready with his shovel. He leans over, holding his shovel, and waits, like a hockey player waits for the referee to drop the puck.

The laneway man never pays attention to anything except his laneway.

If a dinosaur came ripping up Anderson and stopped at the end of the laneway man's laneway and screamed at him, the laneway man would not look up. He would keep shoveling.

All the time the crowd was piling up about three doors down from him, and the police sirens were howling and barking, and a dead man lay bleeding, the laneway man didn't even look over, didn't even glance up!

I'm like the laneway man.

I haven't seen a thing.

I turn the corner.

Sure enough, there's Detective Kennedy's car, waiting, pumping frozen clouds around itself. Clouds of condensation that now hide me.

I get in the car.

"Smart boy," says Detective Kennedy. "I didn't want anybody to see us talking. You never know. The person you think you saw might be right around us somewhere, as we speak!"

My brain is suddenly on fast forward.

If that's true, then when he finds out there's a witness, he'll know it's me. He might come after me. Get me. Like Dumper Stubbs tried to do. Get rid of me before I can identify him. And what if he remembers me from the Hong Kong Beauty Salon? What if he saw that day, Connie Pan and me, laughing at him while he was drooling in the mirror over his hair? What if his memory puts both our faces in a picture that he can see any time he wants? Maybe Connie Pan knows the guy's name! Where he lives, maybe. What if he tries to hurt Connie so she can't identify him? What if he tries to get rid of her? What if he kills both of us?

Or, maybe he didn't see me at all. Didn't see me because of my brown coat up against the brown doors to my yard. Maybe he looked right through me. Maybe he thinks there are no witnesses. But then, if they put my name in the paper again, maybe he'll...

Or maybe he's watching right now like Detective Kennedy says, and then if the paper comes out and says there's a witness, he'll know who it is. Come after me, after Connie Pan...

I don't want to be a hero anymore.

I've got enough self-esteem…

I'm not telling you, Detective Marilyn Kennedy, not telling anybody…

Detective Kennedy

But you *said* you saw some*body*.

Enough Self-Esteem Sweetgrass

I said I saw *something*.

D.K.

I heard you say some*body*.

E.S.E.S.

Some*thing*. A brown van. Tinted windows.

D.K.

And a rifle?

E.S.E.S.

The barrel.

D.K.

And you didn't see who was in the van?

E.S.E.S.

Tinted windows.

D.K.

License plate?

E.S.E.S.

Too much steam around, I guess. Condensation. Clouds. Hard to see anything.

D.K.

You could see in the windows?

E.S.E.S.

Tinted windows, I told you.

D.K.

You said somebody. I heard you. You said you saw somebody!

E.S.E.S.

No, I didn't. I said something. I saw the brown van. The gun coming out the hole in the back. I told you. That's what I saw.

D.K.

You said you saw someone. Someone. One!

E.S.E.S.

I didn't say that.

D.K.

Why are you changing your mind? What are you afraid of?

E.S.E.S.

I'm not changing my mind. I'm not afraid of anything!

She opens her big blue eyes so wide I almost fall in. Hard to lie to big eyes.

Detective Kennedy, relaxing now. Taking it easy.

D.K.

OK, Mr. Sweetgrass. You can get out of the car now. Sweetgrass. Nice name. Native?

E.S.E.S.

Abo. My father is, was, Ojibway. He's dead now,

D.K.

I'm sorry. Perhaps we can talk again sometime?

E.S.E.S.

Whatever.

D.K.

Thanks for your cooperation. So far. Take this card. My number is on it.

E.S.E.S. (To himself.)

She knows I'm lying. Where'd she get eyes like that, anyway?

The sound of the crack of a rifle scares me so much I jump right out of my seat.

"What's wrong?" says my friend Dink the Thinker, and I realize I'm at his house watching TV and that the crack of the rifle is really Dink's dad starting one of his Olympic-caliber coughs.

"Nothing," I say. "Nothing at all."

"You seem so jumpy," says Dink. "And lost. You've been going around all day like somebody's put a spell on you!"

The rest of what Dink says I can't hear because his dad's working very hard at trying to cough up one of his lungs.

Meanwhile, wait, Spud Sweetgrass, and keep your mouth shut tight! Maybe all this will just go away.

V

....

Before I go home, Dink and I have a little chat about our latest project. Dink wants to win the Nobel Prize for science in the year 2025. Dink always thinks ahead. One of the ways he's getting himself ready is he's teaching himself how to write scientifically. The English teachers at Ottawa Tech don't know how to teach people to write scientifically. They only know how to teach people to write about what they did on their summer holidays. So, Dink is teaching himself and I'm helping him.

Dink says the hardest thing to write is to explain how to do an ordinary little job. Like tying your shoe, for instance. Dink likes to try to write down exactly what you should do if you were from another planet and you wanted to know, step by step, how humans tie their shoes.

This week, Dink is working on how to use a can opener. Explain how to work a can opener.

My part of the project is to read what Dink writes, try out exactly what it says, and see if it works.

In Dink's kitchen I try it out on a can of enriched vegetable juice, extra nutrition added, for health nuts only! There's a picture of a really healthy guy on the label. We're opening the can for Dink's dad, the chain-smoking health nut. If they had Dink's dad's picture on this can of juice, nobody would buy it, and not only that, the health department would probably close down the company!

"Grasp opener with left hand and open handles sufficiently to place cutting wheel over rim of can." What if you're left-handed? Never mind. "Close handles firmly and turn crank clockwise to pierce lid. Continue turning until lid is almost cut out, at which time, lid will tilt up slightly."

Everything's working great.

Dink's dad comes in and takes a coughing fit into the enriched vegetable juice.

I was going to have a glass of this stuff but not now.

"At this point, stop turning and remove opener

from can by opening handles. Bend back lid of can and remove contents."

Works perfect.

Good scientific writer, this Dink. This future Nobel Prize winner.

Another project we have is to get Dink's dad off the weed. This project is not working very well. Dink wants to get him addicted to something else, some hobby or something, so he can get his mind off cigarettes. Or doctors. Maybe doctors could help.

Dink says that he thinks acupuncture might be worth a try. Or, he's heard that people can get hypnotized off cigarettes. Maybe being in a hypnotized trance would be a whole lot better than being addicted to cigarettes.

We decide to discuss it later and I head for home.

Down Eccles Street through the cold. It's minus 33, a record, and the wind is whipping around making the temperature with the wind-chill factor minus 47.

Across Booth Street, past the IGA where my mom and I shop, and down Anderson. There's snow in the air but it's not snowing. It's so cold the streetlights look like they're going to give up.

The laneway man is in his laneway chasing the blowing snow. The poor laneway man. I wonder how he got so crazy.

One time Dink and I tried to talk to the laneway man. Dink told him it isn't true that every single snowflake is different, the way we always learned in school. There are snowflakes exactly the same, Dink told him, but you need a computer to find them. He also told the laneway man that the average snowflake fall in Canada is 21 trillion trillion or something. Anyway, it's the number 21 followed by 21 zeros. That's how many snowflakes come down on Canada in a year. That Dink! The stuff he knows!

The laneway man never even looked up. You'd think he would, just this once, since snowflakes are probably his favorite subject.

I walk past the yellow police ribbon around the parking lot where the frozen blood lies under the snow.

I duck through the brown doors that are the gate to my yard. Doors that have been there since horses were used in Ottawa, more than fifty years ago.

Doors I stood there leaning on when a man in a tinted window looked right at me.

But did he see me?

My mom is home late from work.

She's been working overtime at her job at the multicultural center on Somerset Street. She's been working hard to help a family of new Canadians.

The family's doing OK, except for the grandfather.

The problem is they can't get him to come out from under his bed. He crawled in under there last summer in the middle of a big thunderstorm. I remember that storm. It was last July. I was in my chipwagon on Somerset Street, parked in front of the Mekong Grocery.

It was a great storm!

It fit right in with the last movement of Beethoven's Fifth Symphony, which I had cranked up full blast on my wagon stereo.

The old man has been under his bed, off and on, for six months. He's afraid of being struck by lightning.

See, back in his country, every year, more than two hundred people get fried by lightning. It's the worst place in the world for that kind of thing. My mom looked the whole thing up in the library.

When she told the old man's daughter to tell him that, in Canada, not even a dozen people a year die because of lightning, the old man got it wrong when it was translated. He thought my mom said that twelve people were electrocuted right on Somerset Street every day because of lightning.

My mom felt bad because she made things worse when she was only trying to help. The old man was halfway out from under the bed but crawled right back when he got the wrong translation.

The daughter says the old man is so confused that he now thinks that it's my mom who is causing the lightning.

I'm wishing my father was here to listen to my mom tell this.

He would laugh. My mom, the cause of lightning! That's a good one. "She's caused sparks to fly," he might say, "but never lightning, not since I've known her, anyway!"

I like it when my mom tells me stuff that's happening to her.

It makes me want to tell her about things that I'm doing.

But I can't. I'm not telling anybody about who saw or who didn't see.

I'm going to just let it go away.

My mom is looking at me.

She knows something's going on.

My mom has brown eyes with green flecks floating.

When the green flecks start flashing, I can tell that she knows that there's something going on.

Sorry, Mom. Can't tell you. I've decided.

That's it. That's all!

VI

....

Mademoiselle Tarte au Sucre is telling us stuff in French about speaking French. We're talking about speaking of love and romance to your girlfriend or your boyfriend. At least, that's what I think we're talking about. But you never know. My French isn't very good. We might be talking about what Tarte au Sucre had for breakfast this morning.

Now we're going to have our conversation game. We work in pairs. Our topic is supposed to be romance. If we had any girls in the class it would be a bit easier. Since there are no girls, Tarte au Sucre sets it up so that one guy plays the girl for five minutes and then we switch.

Tarte au Sucre rings this little bell she has to tell us when the five minutes is up.

We're supposed to be on a date, having a fancy dinner with candles and music. We're supposed to be saying romantic things to each other because we're madly in love.

It's one of the dumbest things Tarte au Sucre gets us to do.

And the little bell she rings drives everybody wild.

A couple of guys on the other side of the room don't want to be girls, even for five minutes, and a fight almost breaks out before a guy they call Fabio gets things settled down. Fabio is a monster who's been on steroids since about grade six. Fabio says that the two guys who don't want to be girls even for five minutes are now going to be girls for as long as he says they're going to be girls and that's it, that's all! And if they don't like that, then Fabio will stuff them inside their own desks!

I wind up partners with a guy named Roddy. Roddy's idea of something really hilarious is making imitation dicks out of anything he can find and passing them around the room. This is his one and only joke. Making dicks out of anything he can find.

Even Fabio doesn't think this is funny after about the tenth time. And Fabio's idea of funny is to take something out of his nose and go around and show it to everybody.

Right now, I'm playing the girl and Roddy's got a

lot of paper rolled up, and he's got a big eraser from graphic arts taped to the end of the roll. Our whole romantic conversation in French for five minutes is him waving this thing at me. I keep looking out the open classroom door. I'm hoping Connie Pan doesn't walk by in the hall and see us.

When Tarte au Sucre's little bell goes off and it's time to switch, Roddy passes the rolled-up paper with the eraser taped to the end of it over to me.

Everybody's doing Tarte au Sucre's bell. The classroom sounds like a bell factory. Guys are doing little tinkly bells, other guys are doing big bong-bong bells. It's like all the bells on Parliament Hill all of a sudden blew a circuit and they all went berserk.

A guy they call Robin, because he's always imitating Robin Williams, runs around the room covering his ears and dragging his leg, as though the bells are driving him crazy. He's pretending he's a hunchback. "The bells! The bells!" he's yelling.

Mademoiselle Tarte au Sucre is following him around the room, saying stuff in French to him. Probably trying to get him back in his seat.

I take Roddy's imitation dick and crumple it all up into a ball and walk up to the front of the room and dump it into the wastebasket.

When I get back to my desk I can tell that Roddy,

the world's greatest comedian, isn't in a very good mood. He's giving me one of those phony you're-a-dead-man looks that he's got from watching serial-killer videos.

His face is in a twist. He hasn't quite got the look perfected yet. It might be just gas. I look back.

I've got a new look now that works pretty good. I use it on Roddy.

My look says, "I come from a part of town where they shoot people, dead, right under my bedroom window, pal!"

Dink the Thinker once told me that millions of years ago, when humans started walking upright instead of on all fours like animals, we got cooler because the sun's rays didn't strike such a large surface area of our bodies. Therefore we didn't need thick pelts of fur to shield us from the sun and we became naked. Because we needed less water, we developed this super cooling system, very efficient, and then our brains were able to grow larger than any other animal's.

Like a computer, the better cooling system you have, the bigger computer you can build, the bigger brain you can have.

I often wonder, when I look at Roddy, what went wrong.

Somewhere between walking naked on his hind legs and developing a brain, he missed out.

I keep watching the hallway and sure enough, Connie Pan walks by.

The difference between Connie Pan and Roddy is the same as the difference between a butterfly and a cockroach, a goddess and a worm.

I leave Mademoiselle Tarte au Sucre's class and catch up with Connie Pan in the hall. That's the kind of a teacher Tarte au Sucre is. She doesn't know if you're there or if you're not there.

Connie Pan is an A student. Her main course is graphic arts. She's a terrific printer and drawer.

Last year, during a volleyball game she organized on Westboro Beach, she printed each player's name and country by hand on pieces of cloth and tied the cloth like an apron around each player's waist.

Everybody thought the printing was done by a professional. Even long names of new Canadians like Somasundaram Selvakumaram of Sri Lanka looked professional when done by the delicate but strong hands of Connie Pan.

Connie also takes welding.

She wants to be a famous sculptor.

She'll draw her art first on the drafting board. Then she'll sculpt it by welding pieces of metal together.

She's already won a prize in her class for a sculpture

she did. She made a running man out of a coathanger and welded him onto a bicycle wheel rim. Then she welded a loonie onto the wheel.

When you spin the wheel, it looks like the man is chasing the loonie. But he never catches it.

She printed the word "Unemployment" under her sculpture.

She's also a student volunteer for the E.S.L. department. E.S.L. stands for English as a Second Language. She helps the E.S.L. teachers organize stuff for the new Canadians to do, so they can feel better about being in a strange land.

Some of them have never seen snow before, never felt the freezing cold.

"Imagine in your brain," says Connie, "how afraid they might be, when it is a record temperature of minus so many degrees!"

This week she has a different project, though. She's trying to teach a guy to read. But the guy is not an E.S.L. guy. This guy is not a new Canadian. He's not from some foreign country. He's from Ottawa. From Westboro!

The English teachers at Tech can't teach him to read because they only teach English to people who can already read.

And the E.S.L. teachers can't teach him to read

because he's not from a foreign country. They only teach foreigners, new Canadians, how to read.

So, let Connie Pan give it a try...

This kid's problem is he can only read a word if the picture of the word is there beside it.

For instance, if there's a picture of a chicken, and then the word "chicken," he can read the word. But if you give him the word "chickadee" without a picture of a chickadee, he thinks the word is "chicken."

Big problem.

Connie Pan figures that he's got to be taught how to sound out letters, not pick out pictures, if he's ever going to get anywhere.

We're sitting in the cafeteria and I'm having fun watching Connie trying to help this poor guy. Jimmy Smith's his name.

She's sounding out different letters and combinations.

She's getting him to sound out the letters CH. "Ch! Ch!" says Connie.

Dink the Thinker has a book of anatomy at his place. I was looking through it the other day. Looking at the names of different parts of the body. I was looking for one special part.

I'm looking at that body part right now. I'm looking at Connie Pan's philtrum.

I'm watching her philtrum, the way it moves when she pronounces the sounds for poor Jimmy Smith. Getting him to read out the letters CH.

Connie Pan has the most beautiful philtrum on the planet Earth.

The philtrum is that groove in the center of your upper lip, just under your nose.

I want to kiss her there.

And I want to tell her the terrible secret I have.

But I can't.

One thing I'm glad of, though.

I didn't tell Detective Kennedy anything.

I didn't tell her that I saw the man, and more than once. That I saw him where Connie Pan works, at the Hong Kong Beauty Salon. And I didn't tell Detective Kennedy that Connie Pan would even be a better witness than I am.

I didn't tell her that Connie Pan has been close enough to the guy who drove the killer van to have her beautiful hands on his awful head.

That she probably even knows his name!

I'll protect you, Connie!

I watch Connie's philtrum and feel fear and loneliness.

VII

It's so cold that nobody looks at anybody as they walk down Somerset Street. People look straight ahead. And people don't move their bodies much when they walk. They walk kind of stiff in the legs and arms. Some people are so far inside their clothes that you can't see them at all. All you see is clothes walking down Somerset Street.

Dink the Thinker and Connie Pan and me, we're going down to the acupuncture clinic to get Dink's dad an appointment. He's going to get acupunctured to see if that will help him quit smoking.

"We could set a record today!" says Dink through his scarf. The three of us, we're completely covered except for our eyes. Dink and I look like bandits.

Connie is also completely covered except for her eyes. She doesn't look like a bandit, though. She looks more like a mysterious, beautiful Muslim woman, thinking about things, you never know what, behind her veil.

"We're going for the coldest capital city in the world," says Dink. "The coldest capital, up to now, is Ulan Bator, the capital of Mongolia. They figure it out by averaging the daily low temperatures for the month of January. Ulan Bator's record is minus 21 degrees for the month of January. That record was set years ago. We're going for it this year. Today is a record cold for this day in Ottawa. It's minus 33 degrees. With the wind chill it's minus 46 degrees. But they don't count wind chill. If we moved the Parliament Buildings to a place called High Level, Alberta, we'd set a record they'd never match. Minus 46.1 degrees!"

"I don't want to go there," says Connie. Connie always gets an A in Canadian geography. She knows where High Level, Alberta, is on the map. Connie loves some of the names of Canadian towns and cities. She thinks they are hilarious. She collects them in a list. She plans on doing a sculpture of some of them one day. Like Eyebrow, Saskatchewan, and Big Hole, New Brunswick.

The sun is a dead star in the blue sky.

You can't see into the shops on Somerset Street

because the windows are totally covered by a coat of thick frost in beautiful shapes like jungle ferns.

Connie Pan stops in front of the Mekong Grocery and traces the jungle ferns of frost with her mitt.

Someday she will sculpt beautiful shapes like this.

Inside the Mekong Grocery, the noodles are safely stacked on the warm shelves.

Last summer it was very hot here in front of the Mekong Grocery.

A chipwagon blew up here.

It was hotter than hell that day.

Today it's so cold that even though there's lots of traffic noise and wind noise, the noisiest, loudest racket is the crunching of our feet. The crunching, squeezing, creaking, squeaking, squealing of the frozen solid snow under our feet.

It's so cold that the Weather Channel shows complete red alert and a whole list of safety hints and dangers about freezing your skin in ten seconds and not driving out of the city in your car without packing the following things: extra clothes, food, water, flashlight and a candle and some matches. "A simple candle in a stalled vehicle can keep you from freezing to death until help comes," the TV says, over and over again.

Many people will be injured and some will be killed this week by the cold.

All up and down the side streets there are tow trucks, people standing around with jumper cables, other people leaning under the hoods of cars.

And clouds of swirling fog from roaring engines.

The cars look like strange animals with mouths open waiting to be fed on a farm on some frozen planet — not this one!

We're heading down to the acupuncture clinic.

We decided to get serious about this project to save Dink's dad from killing himself smoking cigarettes. We decided the day he had his picture in the paper.

A few weeks ago we open the paper and there's Dink's dad!

In the picture he's sitting in a mall on a ledge in front of some plants. He's smoking a cigarette, of course. He looks awful. There's another guy sitting beside him. He is also by himself. Smoking. Dink's dad is on his morning break from his government job in the passport office.

His office is above the fancy mall they call 240 Sparks uptown near the Parliament Buildings. The civil servants aren't allowed to smoke in their offices so they go down to this mall and smoke.

The story in the paper beside the picture is about a fancy ladies silk-underwear-and-skimpy-pajama store that had to close down because of the cigarette smoke that floated up every day from the hundreds of civil servants smoking their cigarettes down there on their break.

The paper says the fancy underwear and skimpy silk pajamas hanging in the shop got to smell so bad of cigarette smoke that nobody would buy any of them and the store went bankrupt.

The owner of the store says in the paper that people who smoke should be taken out and shot and that she's bankrupt because of them.

The picture in the paper, right beside the story, makes it look like it's these two guys in the picture who are to blame and that they are the ones that should be shot.

"It's not just my fault her underwear is full of smoke!" Dink's dad says. "And I don't even know this other guy!"

Not too long after that, the mall bans all smoking, and now Dink's dad has to go outside and smoke.

Dink's afraid his dad's going to freeze to death out there.

That's why we're going down to the acupuncture clinic to get him an appointment. Get him to quit smoking altogether. That's it, that's all.

Connie Pan is telling us the names of more Canadian places she looked up in the atlas. The names of places that make her laugh, like Gold Bottom in the Yukon Territory, and Jenny's Nose in Newfoundland.

Just as we're turning to go up the stairs of the house where the acupuncture clinic is, I see something across the street that makes my heart stop.

It's a man walking.

The only person out today without a hat.

The hair is big, black and perfect.

The face is tanned. The eyebrows bushy.

Terror runs through me.

I tell Dink and Connie Pan to go ahead in. I tell them I forgot to phone my mom at work about something. I tell them I'll go back up Somerset to the pay phone on the corner. I tell them I'll be back in a minute.

I run up Somerset all the way to Booth Street. The arctic air is freezing in my lungs. I pull my scarf right up over my nose and pull my toque down so that there's just a tiny slit that I can see through.

I cross Somerset Street and start walking back down.

He's easy to spot because he has no hat and the sun is glittering off his shiny, perfect hair. The wind is whipping a bit, blowing people's coats and scarves. But his hair doesn't move.

Probably frozen stiff.

He's getting closer.

His face is square. His jaw is blue.

Closer.

His face is tanned, eyes wide apart.

Closer.

His breath clouds his face, then clears. Just like when he came into focus through the tinted window of the murder van.

His eyebrows are thick and almost meet each other over his nose. His forehead juts over his small black eyes.

His lips are carved, like out of wood. His jaw is clenched, making his face hard.

He walks with a roll, his head up, looking around, his arms swinging free. It's like he doesn't realize it's minus 33 degrees, in the second-coldest capital city in the world. He has no earmuffs, no scarf, no hat. His beautiful, expensive coat is open at the neck. His gloves are tight and smooth looking. But not warm, probably.

His ears are blue from the cold but the tips of his ears are white. They're starting to freeze.

"Look at my hair, everybody!" he seems to be saying. "Look at me!"

We pass each other.

I feel funny. There's something very wrong with

me. I'm going to fall down maybe. Now I realize what it is.

I'm not breathing!

Breathe, Spud, breathe!

I cross the street again and head back down to the acupuncture clinic. I glance back. He's gone. Must have gone in somewhere. The Mekong Grocery, maybe. The video store, maybe. To get warm.

Thaw out his ears.

All of a sudden I'm not sure. Was it him?

Wasn't there something missing? Is that what he looked like? Is that the same guy? The guy I wouldn't tell Detective Kennedy about? I won't tell anybody about?

I lied right into her large blue eyes when she said, "What are you afraid of?" and I looked away from those eyes, and I looked back into them and I lied and I said, "I'm not afraid of anything!"

Dink and Connie Pan come out of the acupuncture clinic. They've got the appointment for Dink's dad.

While we're walking up Somerset Street, I pretend to laugh, and while I'm doing this phony laugh I say to Connie Pan, "Remember that funny guy who loves his hair so much he's always looking in the mirror? Your customer?"

She looks at me. Blank at first. Then, oh, yes, she remembers. Smile.

Then me.

"Well, I just saw him. Walking up the street. He wasn't wearing a hat. Wants everybody to see his hair, I guess!"

"How did his hair look today?" Connie Pan asks.

"His hair? It looked great. Big and shiny. And probably frozen solid!" I laugh.

"I hope he's happy," says Connie Pan. Happy. I love to watch her talk. The way she says the word, happy. "He was very worried yesterday when I did his hair. He wanted to know if it was very charming with his new face!"

She saw him yesterday? She put her hands in his hair, talked, laughed with this guy just yesterday? The idea makes my knees weak.

"His new face?" I say.

"Yes, his new face," says Connie, giggling like a little bell. "Oh, he looks sooo charming now that he has shaved away his little mustache!" Shaved away.

Connie giggles some more.

"What a big change, eh, Spud?" she says.

That was it. That's what was missing. That little mustache that looked like it was drawn on with a pencil.

"Many women will be in love with him now," says Connie Pan, laughing again about her funniest customer. "He will be the talk of the ball!"

Talk of the ball.

Funny, alright.

Funny as a bullet in your back!

VIII

···

You can start at the Arts Center, at the downtown end of the canal, and you can skate up the canal all the way to Dow's Lake. You can take off your skates there and get a free bus back, down Colonel By Drive along the canal, to where you started at the Arts Center. If it's not too cold, you can hang around Dow's Lake and look at all the snow and ice sculptures before you hop on the free bus.

Or you can do the whole thing the other way around.

Connie Pan is planning this for a group of E.S.L. students. It's part of a project she started to make new Canadians feel better about being stuck in a strange country all of a sudden.

Last summer she organized a volleyball game on Westboro Beach which was a big hit. The best part of the game was Connie Pan made them play the whole game without a net and without a ball. Everybody enjoyed it.

While she's telling me about the skating trip she's planning, I start asking her how you say the word "canal" in Vietnamese. She's showing me how to say "canal" and I'm putting my face right up to hers and I'm touching her philtrum, very gently, with my finger. I'm trying very hard to say it like she says it but it doesn't sound right.

Then I say Colonel By in front of the word. Colonel By was an Englishman, an engineer, who built the canal more than 150 years ago. The driveway that runs along his canal is named after him. They should have named his canal after him, too. He built it, didn't he? Instead, they call it the Rideau Canal.

Did he ever dream, in his wildest dreams, that a boy, half Abo and half Irish and half a whole lot of other things, would be teasing a girl, who was half Chinese and half Vietnamese, about how to say what his canal was?

"Colonel By *sông dào*," I say very slow.

Then Connie says it again, very slow.

I press my finger gentle on her upper lip and say it very slow.

She has her two perfect hands on my face and she's pressing my cheeks together so my lips pout out. I must look like a fish.

"Spuddy," she whispers, "I like you."

We're standing outside the guidance office at Ottawa Tech. Connie Pan has walked me down here. The Cyclops wants to see me for some reason. Usually I only have to see The Cyclops once every two weeks. If you get kicked out of school you have to report to guidance every two weeks and get guided. It's sort of like being on parole. They check on you, see what you're up to. See how long it's going to be before you're hoofed out again.

See what further horrible crimes you're committing these days.

In the display case outside the guidance office, The Cyclops has pinned up my picture from the newspaper last summer. Under the picture is the headline about John "Spud" Sweetgrass, hero. It's nearly half a year ago that was in the paper. Every time I go by the guidance office I see it there.

Every time I go to see The Cyclops I ask him will he please take that picture down.

But he won't. It's still there, locked inside the display case, pinned up on the board.

Now, while Connie Pan and John "Spud" Sweetgrass, hero, have a hold of each other's faces right outside the guidance office, out comes The Cyclops.

His eye is like a laser beam on me.

I think he means it's time to let go of Connie Pan's philtrum and go into his office.

Here I go. What now, I wonder.

The police called. A Detective Kennedy. She was asking about Sweetgrass. What kind of a kid is he, she wanted to know. Reliable? Honest? Ever been in trouble?

The Cyclops goes on.

"The police — she — told me you were the one who called in that gang murder on Rochester Street. Did that happen very near your place?"

"Right next door."

"And you saw…"

"I saw a van. A brown van. I told the police."

"And you saw a rifle…"

"Yeah, I told her that."

"And you didn't see anything else…"

"No." What's going on here? Is The Cyclops working for the cops now?

Looking into The Cyclops' eye and lying is almost

as bad as telling lies into the big blue eyes of Detective Kennedy.

"Why does she think you saw more than what you told her? Why does she think you're holding something back?" says The Cyclops.

"I don't know…"

If you look *beside* the one eye, look at his *ear*, for instance, it's quite a bit easier.

Or at the sign he has on his desk. "Same-Day-Service-Sullivan," the sign says. The Cyclops' real name is Mr. Sullivan. The sign means that when The Cyclops says he'll let you know about something soon, he'll let you know that same day. This is true about The Cyclops. If he says he'll do something, he'll do it. Not like a lot of teachers. A lot of teachers say they're going to do something for you and the next time you see them, they don't even remember your name.

"I have a theory," says The Cyclops. "The police are desperate to solve this string of underworld crimes. They'll put pressure wherever they think…they'll squeeze anybody and everybody they can, where there's the slightest hope of new information…"

It sounds like The Cyclops is on my side. This is a switch.

"That was courageous of you to phone in what you saw. It must have been terrifying. Seeing someone gunned down in cold blood like that. You know, many people would have chosen silence, would rather not have been involved…leave-it-to-the-other-guy type of attitude…"

"I guess so. I don't know," I say, feeling a load of compliments coming on. Another big number to build up my self-esteem. That's the way they work. They blow you right up and then tell you what they really wanted to tell you in the first place. Which is usually that you're doing something wrong.

After this build-up, he's going to tell me that I'd better tell the rest of what I saw, because they're going to find out anyway and then it will be worse for me, etc., etc.

Here it comes.

"I just wanted to see you to tell you that they — she — called and that I gave them — her — a very positive report on you. That's all I wanted to share with you. Keep me posted, as they say, that is, if you wish…and if you need any help, anybody to talk to, everything is, as they say, confidential here. Thanks for dropping by…"

Is that it? Is that all? Where's the part where he tells me that what I'm doing is wrong?

I get up to leave. This is the easiest guidance visit I've ever had.

This Cyclops, this Same-Day-Service-Sullivan, guidance guy with the one eye, he seems all right. It almost feels good, the way he's talking.

Now, some more.

"My grandfather," he says, "was Métis. Part Cree Indian, as it were. He used to say that if you had a secret and you were stuck with it and it was burning inside of you, so to speak, he used to say that you should dig a hole in the ground around where you live and say the secret into the hole, at midnight, and then replace the earth into the hole exactly as it was. And if you did that, the old people used to say, you'd feel a whole lot better…*whole* lot — no pun intended, Spud, my boy!"

I guess I'm standing there with my mouth open.

Now I guess I'm back out in the hall.

There's nobody around. Connie Pan's gone somewhere.

The Cyclops has Abo blood! And that thing about the hole. Why didn't I remember that? My father told me that once. And I completely forgot about it until now.

In fact, The Cyclops, for a second or two there, almost sounded like my father. "If you had a secret and you were stuck with it and it was burning inside of you…" That's the kind of way my father would put it.

On the way home I'm thinking about my father's ax. I think I know where it is, under all that old furniture in the back shed.

I turn off Wellington and head up Nanny Goat Hill which is Booth Street. It's so cold, it's hard to breathe. Maybe Dink the Thinker is right. Maybe this year we will win the championship as the world's coldest capital city. Beat out whatsit, the capital of Mongolia. Or is it Libya? No, that's the hottest. Dink told us that last summer.

The cold makes you sleepy.

A homeless man drops spit in a long string from his mouth. It's frozen by the time it hits the ground!

I have a short chat with my mom about the old guy who won't come out from under his bed, and then I tell her I'm tired and I'm going to bed early. She gives me a funny look.

I'm getting to be a pretty good liar. Or, am I?

The tired part isn't a lie because I am tired, but that's not why I'm going to bed early. I'm going to bed early because I have to get up early. Real early.

I set my clock for eleven-thirty.

I have to be wide awake by midnight.

IX

....

My alarm wakes me at eleven-thirty. The Weather Channel is completely red. WARNING. The temperature is minus 35. A record for this day. Forecast: clear and extremely cold.

Out on Rochester Street, car engines are revving and roaring, wheels are spinning, guys are shouting. It's the gang coming out of the Village Inn across the street. Everybody's out trying to start everybody else's car.

Billows of exhaust and condensation. You can hardly see the sign "The Village Inn" through the clouds coming from the cars and the drunks trying to start the cars.

Hoods are open, tow trucks' lights are spinning like

searchlights, lit flashlights are falling into the snow-banks, cables are tangled, golden sparks are shooting from batteries, guys are falling, cursing, laughing, women are screaming, starters are whirring, doors are slamming, horns are blowing, rubber is screaming on the ice as hard as steel, tools are ringing, and two cars that are stuck together are ripping each other's bumpers off.

I get a square shovel and find my father's ax in the shed bchind a bunch of junk. The blade of my father's ax is rusted. When I see the rust I feel ashamed and sad.

He used to keep it sharp and shiny.

Once, when we were out camping, I held up the ax, like a mirror, while my father trimmed his own hair with his hunting knife.

I'm in my yard, which is closed in by buildings on all sides and is quiet. The brown doors lead into the street. Out there they shoot you dead from brown vans. The doors are shut and locked.

The light from my bedroom window is yellow. I can see the warm, fancy shapes of the thick frost on the panes.

It gives me enough light to do my work. I'm like a midnight gravedigger on a stage in a play I saw once.

Except it wasn't minus so many degrees.

Minus so many degrees!

Thinking of Connie Pan makes me warm.

I brush away the top layer, the feathery, dusty snow, to get down to the stiff crust. This crust is thick and strong enough to hold me. If I jumped hard on it I could break through but I don't want to. Too messy. This has to be done right. I set my tools down side by side on the crust and clear off a perfect square about the size of a trap door.

It's so cold that you can't feel it. This is the cold to look out for.

There's no wind, no breeze, perfectly still, the sky is clear of cloud. It's filled with a quarter moon and a billion stars. The Weather Channel says this is the most dangerous time of all. When it's pleasant, beautiful like this.

When everything is nice and cozy. That's when they get you. For instance, after you've had a nice couple of cups of your favorite coffee, and then you stroll out to your brand-new warm car.

When it's like this, you could decide to sit down for a little rest, take a look at the big show in the sky up there, feel really great, lie back a bit, just for a minute, maybe take a little snooze…and wake up dead…frozen stiff as a popsicle!

With the square shovel I'm careful. I cut four sides of a perfect square the size of a trap door.

I slide the shovel under the square from each side and loosen the hard crust from the snow underneath.

When it's free, I carefully lift the square of crust off the snow and set it down away from the work area where it won't be damaged.

It's out in the shadow now, where I can't see it.

I shovel out the next layer. This layer is lumpy snow, icy, coarse, breaks into funny shapes, isn't too heavy. It goes down pretty deep, to half the length of the handle of my shovel.

With my father's ax, I chop out the next layer, which is milky-colored hard ice and is about two hands deep. Under the ax it breaks up like thick hard glass chunks and they clunk together like lumps of marble.

I clean out these pieces with my hands, like a dog digging.

I keep this pile separate from the pile of coarse icy snow.

The next layer is packed snow. Because the hole is as deep as the shovel length now, the work is getting harder. I stack this snow in a separate pile.

My head and my hands are starting to sweat. I check my alarm clock, which I have brought down and placed on the doorstep leading into my back shed.

It looks lonely there, in the shadows, propped up in the snow. Can clocks freeze?

It's five minutes to midnight.

The hole is down to frozen grass. I can feel it.

Now the hard part.

I lie on my stomach. I have to lean way in to get any kind of decent whack at the frozen grass with the ax. I try putting the shovel into the hole and using it to support my left hand while I chop with my right. It's hard, sweaty work.

I stop to rest. Nice and pleasant to have a short rest on such a beautiful night.

I roll over and look at the sky shining, glittering with silver points and the moon looking cozy in the cold.

Nice to have a rest like this after shoveling and chopping. Head sweaty. Hands hot. Maybe loosen the scarf. Take off my toque.

Slip off the mitts for a minute.

Cool off the hands.

Feels good.

Maybe even take a little snooze.

It's nice out here.

Reminds you of summer, camping, sleeping under the stars, on a fishing trip with my father.

Doze off like in Mademoiselle Tarte au Sucre's

French class in the afternoon when the warm sun is streaming in the windows and she's reading to us, like she does every day, the continued story of *Les Misérables* in French, by Victor Hugo. Nobody in the room, except her, knows anything about what's going on in *Les Misérables,* but who cares. It's peaceful and she's got a nice voice. It could be a beautiful love scene by a lake she's reading to us, or it could be a bloody massacre during a war…what's the difference…

So peaceful, her voice going on…

My father, using his ax as a mirror…

Is that a shooting star up there…look at it. Look at the arc…

There's a loud crack! It wakes me up, but I'm not sleeping!

The loud, cracking thud. Came from the old garages, which used to be the stables where they kept the horses more than fifty years ago. The sudden sound is a nail popping in the old wood. It's so cold the nails are shrinking, tearing through the wood.

All of a sudden, I'm in a panic!

I almost went to sleep!

The sweat on my head is frozen!

My hands are white.

I cover up again.

My throat is burning.

My nose is plugged with frost.

What a stupid, stupid…

I try to chop some more of the frozen grass, but it's like chopping concrete. The ax bounces right off. You might as well try to chop a hole in a sidewalk. The ax is ringing. Are those sparks coming off each time I hit? Is the grass in Ulan Bator like cement?

I get up and check the clock.

It's nearly twelve.

It's time.

On my hands and knees I speak down into the hole. The secret.

"I know who the driver of the killer van is. I saw him. I can identify him. Connie Pan knows him. She probably knows his name. I lied to the police. I'm not telling anyone about this. Only you." Talking to a hole. I must be nuts!

Now. Quick!

I shovel back in the last layer, the hard-packed snow.

I replace the layer of thick, heavy, marbly chunks.

I shovel back in the lumpy stuff.

I smooth over the lumps with some regular snow.

I carefully replace the trap door of crust.

I spread the feathery powder over the top.

My alarm goes off. It sounds like it's limping. Too cold for clocks.

Done.

The secret is in the hole.

I pick up the shovel and my father's ax and the clock.

Now, get in the house.

Quick, before you freeze!

Go!

X

....

Dink's dad bought Dink something he's wanted for a long time. A cellular phone. One of the newest ones that fit in your shirt pocket. Dink's dad can't get over how the top flips open and shut. He used to watch the old Star Trek series all the time, the one with Spock and Captain Kirk. He says he never thought that when Captain James T. Kirk used to flip the top back on his communicator when he was finished talking and say, "Kirk out!" that he'd ever see the day when it could actually happen. And now he's just bought one for his son!

"What next?" says Dink's dad.

Dink is trying out his phone, phoning some computer stores, asking them questions about the latest software or something, then, when he's finished talking, he's flipping his phone shut and then his dad is saying, "Say, 'Kirk out!' why don't you? Go ahead, phone somebody else, and then when you're done talking, flip it shut, like Captain James T. Kirk used to, and say, 'Kirk out!'"

So, to please his dad, Dink calls another computer store and asks them how much is a whatdyacallit and then he says, "OK. Thanks. Kirk out!" and flips his phone shut and shoves it in his back pocket.

And Dink's dad bursts out laughing and claps his hands and tries to speak but the laughing makes him start to choke and then he breaks into a coughing fit that would set all the emergency screens off on the bridge of the Starship *Enterprise*.

I like the way Dink and Dink's dad like each other. They're always doing stuff for each other. Like Dink trying to get him to quit smoking cigarettes and his dad buying Dink this cellular phone.

It makes me miss my father.

Dink lets me use his phone to call Connie Pan because my mom wanted me to find out if there was anything Mrs. Pan wanted us to bring over for supper.

Connie Pan's mother asked me and my mom over for early supper. My mom and Mrs. Pan are friends now since they met last summer at the multicultural center. Mrs. Pan sometimes translates for my mom when she's trying to help some new Canadians who speak Chinese.

Mrs. Pan started out not liking me very much. When she found out I got kicked out of school, she didn't like me even worse.

But then, when she got to know my mom and they got to be friends, she started to like me a bit better.

She still calls me Bignose, though. But now when she says it, she's got a tiny little smile to go with it. Mrs. Pan doesn't seem very polite, but my mom says it's just her "manner," and she's a very kind, caring person.

I said we were invited for *early* supper because the Pans always eat at 5:15 and finish about a quarter to six. And then, as soon as you're finished eating, Mrs. Pan says, "OK. Go home now!"

When my father was alive and we'd have some guests over for supper it would take about three hours to eat and at two o'clock in the morning everybody'd still be there.

Last time, over at Mrs. Pan's, I was just swallowing the last of a piece of sweet dessert she'd made when she got up and said, "OK. Go home now!"

I was insulted, so Connie Pan had to explain it to me at the front door while I put on my boots.

She told me that I insulted her mother by leaving! See, when she says, Go home, you're supposed to say, "Oh, no, I'd like to stay longer. It's so enjoyable here!"

While Connie Pan was explaining this and helping me zip up my jacket and put on my mitts and toque and scarf, I heard her mom shout out from the kitchen, "Bignose, he gone home yet?"

I felt like yelling, "No, No-nose, he not!" but I didn't.

Connie Pan just laughed and reached up and tapped me on the nose with her first finger.

I get Connie Pan on the cellular and she tells me that we don't need to bring anything over for supper. She also says that it's lucky I phoned because if we did bring something over, Mrs. Pan would be insulted again.

When my father was alive and people would come over for supper, they always brought something. A chunk of cheese, or a pie or a tin of biscuits or a bottle of wine or a couple of tomatoes from their garden, if it was summer.

Summer. What a word! It doesn't seem possible that there could ever be summer again!

It's not even four-thirty in the afternoon and it's already dark.

I go home to pick up my mom.

It's snowing a bit. On Anderson I stop for a minute to watch the laneway man. His laneway is, as usual, black. He's got the only black laneway in Ottawa. Nobody knows how he does it. Even the city streets, like Rochester Street, which are normally down to pavement because of the salt they put on, are snow-packed. And slippery. The salt can't melt the snow away fast enough before it freezes again. But the laneway man's laneway is right to the black top. The snowbanks on each side are cut square and perfect. Right now, the laneway man is sweeping the few floating-down flakes as they try to land gently on his laneway. He's muffled up so that you can see his breath but not his face. I wave at him but, of course, he doesn't wave back. He never does.

He's only interested in one thing in life.

When my mom and I get to Connie Pan's, Mrs. Pan tells us that Mr. Pan won't be there. Mr. Pan is never there. He's a traveling salesman or something. He's always going to South America or India or China or someplace. I only saw him once. He had four huge trunks and he was trying to get them into a taxi. There was a big argument with the taxi driver about the trunks. One of the trunks was stuck halfway out the back door of the taxi. There was Connie Pan's dad pushing the trunk into the cab and the driver, on the other side of the cab, pushing it out. The driver was an Indian guy wearing a big purple turban. He was yelling in Indian. Mr. Pan was wearing no hat, a black suit and shiny black shoes. He was shouting in Chinese.

They seemed to understand each other pretty well. One wanted the trunk in, one wanted the trunk out. Pretty simple.

My mom and I are wearing so many clothes tonight it gets embarrassing taking them off in Connie Pan's small hallway.

First of all, my boots seem so big that they take up half the hallway. My mom's boots are laced so she has to bend over to get them off. While she's bent over, Mrs. Pan is trying to haul my coat over the top of Mom. My coat weighs a ton and Mrs. Pan staggers backwards with it until Connie helps her lift it up to put on top of the radiator.

Then my mom's coat is next. It's fastened with wooden pegs and while she's undoing those, Connie and Mrs. Pan's hands are there, too, helping to undo the coat. There's thirty fingers in there, undoing a coat. Then the hats and mitts have to be shoved down the sleeves and the scarves handed over and the sweaters and now the hallway of the little house is so full of people and clothes you can hardly move.

Maybe we should stand right here and have supper,

and then we wouldn't have to get all untangled to go into the living room and then the dining room.

Just in time for Mrs. Pan to yell, "OK, go home now!"

We go into the little living room and then into the little dining room and sit down. There's a huge pot steaming in the middle of the table with a flame under it.

We're having Mongolian Fire Pot for supper.

Connie Pan tells me it's called Shua Yang Jou. I like the way she says the Chinese names. I'm careful, though. I don't want Mrs. Pan to catch me looking at Connie's philtrum.

We each have a plate of meat, a small bowl of sauce, chopsticks and a big soup spoon and a napkin.

In the middle of the table is the boiling pot with a flame burning under it.

There's a big bowl of noodles and another big tray of all kinds of funny-looking vegetables and a basket of hot bread.

You pick up a piece of your meat with the chopsticks. The meat is sliced as thin as paper. You rinse the piece around in the boiling broth in the middle of the table. When the thin slice of meat changes color, you pull it out of the hot water, you dip it in the sauce and eat it. Have some hot bread with it.

My first piece of meat is done but it slips out of my chopsticks and I lose it. There it is, floating in the steaming pot. Mrs. Pan sees this, laughs, reaches into the pot with her chopsticks, grabs my piece of meat, dips it in her sauce and eats it! She steals my piece of meat!

It's like she's saying, "Finders keepers, sucker!"

When the meat's all done (Mrs. Pan steals five pieces of mine, altogether), she gets a big ladle and pours some hot broth out of the pot into each of our bowls of sauce and we drink that. If any dribbles down your chin from your bowl, you've got a napkin, use it.

Now she dumps all the noodles and vegetables into the big pot and makes a big vegetable stew and we all share that.

I put extra sauce in mine. Mrs. Pan sees this and points her chopsticks at me and nods her head and smacks her lips like she's saying, "Bignose not such idiot after all!"

We finish up with a big basket of peeled oranges and more hot bread.

It's hot in here! It must be over plus 90 in here. Outside, it's more than minus 30. There's over 120 degrees difference between in here and out there.

Everybody's sweating and the room is full of steam.

Mrs. Pan and Connie, together, blow out the flame that's under the pot.

Mongolian Fire Pot! They must have invented this supper in Mongolia, to get two things done at once. Get full and get warm at the same time.

And another thing. This supper took more than two hours to eat. And that was mostly because people were having so much fun stealing the other guy's food out of the boiling pot. For a while there, both my chopsticks were floating around in the pot. Really hilarious, eh, Mrs. Pan? I was wrong that the Pans always eat in a big hurry. Looks like it's going to be a sit-around-and-relax kind of supper like the ones we used to have at our place.

But, oh, no, here she goes again!

"OK, go home now!" says Mrs. Pan.

"Oh, no," says Mom. "We have some chatting to do. You and I have some culture center business to talk about and Spud and Connie are in the middle of planning a big skating party on the canal, so we would like to stay longer if you don't mind!"

Very smart, my mom.

Then, Mrs. Pan does this amazing thing.

She stands up and looks for a long time at my mom and me.

It's almost like she's going to start to cry. Then she says two words.

"Thank you," she says, and gives this little bow.

My mom, she's got some water in her eyes, too. She gives a little bow. I give a little bow to Connie and her mom.

There's a long, long quiet.

Connie Pan takes me into the little living room through a curtain made of beads and we sit together on a wide chair made for two people. Or maybe it's a small couch where Mr. Pan lies down and takes a snooze, if he's ever home long enough. Anyway, it's either a big chair or a small couch. It jingles a bit when we move in it.

We're talking about the E.S.L. skating party on the canal that Connie is organizing. We're talking about how many of her group have skates, or how to get skates for them. We're talking about how many of the E.S.L.ers can skate, how far they can skate, could any of them go the whole way from Dow's Lake to the Arts Center downtown. We're talking about the weather, the cold, what the E.S.L.ers should wear. We're talking about keeping the group together, how to keep some of them from getting lost. We're talking about safety, about food, about time, about where to start, about getting into groups, about having a test run first, about going at night, during the week, or on the weekend when there'll be almost 100,000 people skating.

There's a lot of heat and steam in Connie Pan's little living room. Steam that floated through the beaded curtain from the fire pot during supper and steam from the conversation Connie Pan and I are having on the little couch.

It's so cozy here. From the other part of the house we can hear my mom and Connie Pan's mom talking and laughing.

On the table in front of the little couch is a pile of papers. Most of them are Chinese.

There's the *Ottawa Citizen*, too.

The front page says something about a killer confessing.

I blink my eyes. I'm swimming up out of a steaming pot of vegetable stew. I pick up the paper.

Connie Pan is talking about tying all the E.S.L. skaters on a long rope...would that be dangerous... would anybody get strangled...

I can't hear what she's saying.

My eyes are clearing.

I'm reading the front page of the *Ottawa Citizen*.
Ottawa Killer Nabbed in U.S.

"Mafia hit man arrested in Florida confesses to Ottawa killing."

"Miami police revealed today that Bruce Mac-Gregor, a known professional hit man, has turned snitch and is expected to give up some big names in the crime business in return for protection and reduced sentences…"

The paper says he's already admitted to over a dozen murders including one in Ottawa, Canada, earlier this week.

Then it says MacGregor stated that he had a local accomplice but that he had no knowledge of his identity.

Then it says this: "Unofficial spokesperson for the Ottawa police suggested that there might possibly be a local reluctant eye witness not identified as yet, who could hasten the arrest of the driver of the van, who is probably from the Ottawa area…"

A reluctant witness…

That's me!

Connie Pan is staring at me.

"What's wrong with you, Spud?"

All of a sudden I feel cold.

XI

....

"A reluctant witness who could possibly soon come forward, unofficial police spokesperson says…"

That's me. The reluctant witness.

And who's the "unofficial police spokesperson"? Is it Detective Kennedy? Probably. I knew she knew I was holding back, lying. My mom knew there was something wrong. The Cyclops knew I was holding tight to a secret. Dink the Thinker knew there was something bothering me. Connie Pan is now looking at me funny.

I'm not as good a liar as I thought.

Maybe I should call a meeting.

They could all meet me in my yard tonight at midnight and I could open up the hole in the snow, let them hear what's in there. "Now hear this," the hole would shout…

Right now Dink the Thinker's telling Connie Pan and me about what happened to his dad at the acupuncture clinic.

We're standing outside Mademoiselle Tarte au Sucre's classroom. I'll stand around here as long as I feel like it because Tarte au Sucre never checks attendance and doesn't know my name, anyway. Dink and Connie have spares.

Dink's telling Connie Pan how acupuncture started in China. It seems funny, when you think of it. Only Dink the Thinker could do a thing like this. Tell somebody from China all about China. If Dink the Thinker was Chinese, he'd probably be going around telling Canadians all about how maple syrup got started.

"Acupuncture started about 4,500 years ago in China. They believed the body was made up of two forces, Yin and Yang…"

Along come Roddy and Fabio, a couple of really exciting intellectuals.

Roddy likes the words Yin and Yang.

"Yin-Yang! Yin-Yang!" says Roddy, who thinks we're talking about something else entirely. He's got his eyes shut and his tongue is slobbering in and out and he's doing a Michael Jackson with his crotch.

"Yin-Yang this!" says Roddy, the world's finest and most intelligent show-business personality and conversationalist.

Connie Pan is side-spying Roddy out of the corners of her eyes, like maybe a poisonous blow-fish is taking a swim near her head. She moves a little closer over to me.

"Hey, Dink!" says Roddy. "Up your Yin-Yang, eh, you know what I mean?"

"Yes, I know what you mean, Roddy, and thanks ever so much for including me in your thoughts," says Dink the Thinker. Dink can be pretty sarcastic sometimes. Dink doesn't even look at him when he says this. As far as Dink is concerned, Roddy is too far down the food chain to pay any attention to.

Now, Fabio wants to talk to me. And I know what he wants to talk about. It's his favorite subject.

"Hey, Spuddo, you know that van, you know, when they whacked that guy, if you see that van around your house, why don't you get a rocket launcher and KA-BOOM! Blow it A-WAY! HA! HA! HA!"

"I saw it this morning, Fabio," I say, "but for some crazy reason, I just didn't happen to have my launcher with me at the time." I can be sarcastic sometimes, too.

"Oh, yeah, right! You got a rocket launcher? Tell me about it! HA! HA! HA!" says Fabio. He must have had a bowl of steroids for breakfast this morning. He's so big and puffed up, he looks like he might burst.

"Well, you're right, Fabio. I haven't got a rocket launcher. You got me there!"

"Hey, Dink," says Fabio. He swells himself up like the Pillsbury Doughboy, "Where'd ya get all the muscles, Dink?"

Dink has about as many muscles as a mop handle.

"Hey, Dink," says Fabio. "How'd you ever get to be such a nerd-dweeb?"

"Have you ever heard of William Gates?" says Dink. He moves over a little closer to me. I can tell he's got a real zinger ready for Fabio. Trouble is, Fabio probably won't even get it.

"Who?" says Fabio. His eyes look a bit glassy. Maybe he had two bowls of "stereos" this morning.

"William 'Bill' Gates," says Dink. "He's a multi-billionaire. He's produced most of the world's computer software. He's one of the planet's most powerful men."

"Yeah. So?" says Fabio.

"Bill Gates is also a nerd-dweeb," says Dink.

"Oh, wow, whoopee-turds!" says Fabio, and body-checks his pal, Roddy, in through Tarte au Sucre's classroom door, and goes in after him. There's a crash as Roddy wipes out on a desk in there. What a mental giant!

"As I was saying," says Dink, "Yin and Yang have to be balanced in the body for you to be healthy. The balance of Chee."

"Chee," says Connie Pan.

"Yes. There are two thousand acupuncture points along the body's meridians that carry Chee through the body. The needles inserted in the right points restore the Chee balance."

"Did your dad get his Chee balanced so he could quit smoking?" I ask.

"No. The acupuncturist put thirty needles into his face, his throat and his chest and his smoking hand. He was OK until they let him look in the mirror. Then he went sort of berserk. He was supposed to leave them in for half an hour. He started ripping them out. They got him calmed down but when they told him he'd have to have this done ten more times, he said forget it and lit up a cigarette. He could hardly get it into his mouth, there were so many needles around."

"Then what happened?" I say.

"They kicked him out. There's no smoking in the acupuncture clinic."

After French class I stroll by The Cyclops' office. Should I go in and tell him everything? Should I go in and call Detective Sullivan from his phone? If the driver of the van sees in the paper that there's a "reluctant witness" who is maybe going to talk, and if the driver saw me that day, and if the driver remembers me and Connie together that day at the beauty salon, and if he decides to…

If, if, if.

And if I tell everything, and if it's all in the paper, and if he decides to get rid of Connie and me so that when he is picked up there won't be any witnesses…

Or if he decides, since they've already got the shooter in Florida, if he decides just to disappear, then it will be all over…maybe.

Or if he decides to get Connie, because she knows him best, then it would be all because of me…

Or if he didn't even see me…and I talked…I'd be telling him who I am and then it would lead to Connie…

If, if, if…

And if my father was here …

If my father was here he'd say, "If you're going to do something, do it all the way!"

If I do tell everything, it could go all wrong. If I don't tell, that could also go all wrong.

It seems like I'm in a trap.

I look into The Cyclops' office. His desk is very neat, with the sign, Same-Day-Service-Sullivan, and his pen and pencil set and his blotter all in place, the lights off...he's not here today.

If he was sitting there, I'd probably walk right in and unload the whole thing on him. Then everything would start happening...

My mind is doing things I can't control. Say, for instance, The Cyclops slipped on the ice and sprained his wrist and had to go to the doctor, and that's why he's not here today. The ice is there because of this record cold spell. The cold spell is in Ottawa because of barometric pressure and movements of air masses. These pressures and movements are caused by the orbits of the planets and the angle of the rays of the sun. The sun is part of a bunch of old explosions a billion years ago in the cosmos which is caused by...I'm starting to sound like Dink the Thinker.

Who's controlling my life, anyway?

A special slippery piece of ice on The Cyclops' steps this morning causes him not to be here, and because he's not here, my life changes...what if he stepped a little to the left or right...and who says he sprained his wrist, anyway?

What am I talking about?

And what if Al Laromano decided he needed to have another cup of coffee that day at Rocco's Cafe? Then I wouldn't have been standing there when he came out. What made him want to leave just when he did? Did he think about staying for one more? What if the waitress flashed her eyes at him, or winked at him? Would he have decided to stay…is all of this happening to me because of a wink of an eye?

If, if, if…

I have to decide something.

I want to tell and I don't want to tell.

That puts me nowhere.

What I have to do is wait. And, while I'm waiting, I might as well do something. Do what? Find out more. Get closer to him.

Outside Ottawa Technical High School, Albert Street is as quiet as a funeral. It's been snowing all day. It's only three-thirty in the afternoon but it's getting dark already. The snow is up to your knees.

And it's another record temperature.

Minus 33 degrees. Not as cold as yesterday but the coldest day on record for this day.

Eat your heart out, Mongolia!

Canada will be the new champ for having the planet's coldest capital city.

And, look out Mr. Van Driver, Mr. Murderer's Helper. Here comes Spud Sweetgrass!

XII

....

Here comes Spud Sweetgrass! Did I say that? Getting brave all of a sudden can be very scary. It's like standing in the middle of the highest diving board when you're a kid. You're standing there trying to figure out if you're going to go or not. Up to now, you've got a choice. You've got a few choices. You can go back. You can hang off the board by your hands and let yourself drop (it's not so high that way). You can stand at the end, close your eyes and step off. You can take a run and jump off. Or you can dive off head first.

Then, all of a sudden, you're going to dive off. There's no way out now. You've done enough just standing there like an idiot. Somehow, inside you, something clicked over, the decision is made. You've decided.

Now, even if you tried to change your mind, you couldn't. You're going, that's it, that's all!

First thing I have to do is get some help.

From Ottawa Tech, I head down Bay Street towards Somerset.

This is a heavy snowfall. There's no wind, not even a breeze. The flakes are thick and close together and come straight down. You can only see about three houses ahead of you. It's like trying to see through Connie Pan's curtain made of beads. Only here, on Bay Street, you're looking through a curtain of white beads, miles thick, as thick as the end of the world.

I'm pushing, wading through snow.

I'm in slow motion.

Everything is silent. The snow muffles everything. The cold numbs everything. A bus goes by but there is no sound. The bus appears, then disappears. You pass by a person walking. The person seems like a ghost in the snow. The windowsills of the houses are plugged with snow. The houses look like nobody lives in them. The bare trees reach up with their branches like claws and then fade away, up into the falling snow.

It's getting darker.

Up ahead, a snow plow speeds down Somerset Street, throwing up a huge curling surf of flying snow. Like a ship, full speed ahead through the foam, a blue light spinning on the mast.

I turn down Somerset, I follow the plow.

It's the kind of snow, the way it's falling, you know it's not going to stop.

I cut down Cambridge Street so I can pass Connie Pan's house. The streetlight just went on in front of her place. In the summer, one night, we sat on her porch and waited for that light to go on. It's hard to catch it. You might blink or look away and miss it going on. I missed it that time but Connie Pan saw it. I missed it because I was looking over at Connie.

She said the light went on so fast she thought she heard it click.

I just saw the streetlight go on now. If it clicked, I didn't hear it. It seemed to go on slowly, like it almost didn't make it. Is it slower because of the snow, the cold?

Or is it me? The whole slow-motion feeling I'm having?

Connie Pan's narrow house sits in the snow, looking out, like a tall, skinny, funny-looking kid with a weird, pointed white hat on.

When I pass the house, I walk backwards for a few

steps, watching the pointed hat until the whole house melts away, vanishes into the storm.

I go down Eccles Street and climb through the snow and into Dink the Thinker's apartment building.

It's hot in here, in Dink's apartment. Dink's dad keeps the heat up too high. By the time I get my clothes off, there's sweat on my face. By the time I get down to my undershirt, there's a pile of clothes on the hall chair, as high as Connie Pan's mother.

I'm going to tell Dink everything.

But I have to wait because Dink is busy.

Dink's got his cellular phone hooked up to his computer and he's calling his contact at CISTI, the Canada Institute of Scientific and Technical Information at the National Research Council. Dink is getting CISTI to show him on his screen everything you want to know about the doomsday comet, Swift Tuttle. Swift Tuttle is the name of a large comet, the size of Chinatown, that is supposedly going to collide with Earth and wipe us all out. It will have the impact force of 1.6 million times the atomic bomb dropped on Hiroshima.

The reason Dink needs information on the doomsday comet, Swift Tuttle, is that Dink's dad is using it as an excuse not to quit smoking. Now that the acupuncture didn't work, Dink's dad is going to give up trying to quit. What's the use of quitting, says Dink's dad, when the doomsday comet, Swift Tuttle, is going to wipe us all out? Might as well smoke all the cigarettes we want, we're all going into the fire, anyway!

Dink has just found out from CISTI that the comet won't hit for at least another 134 years. And even then, the chances are slim.

"Oh, great!" says Dink's dad. "Now I got plenty of time to die of lung cancer!"

Later, alone in the kitchen with Dink, I tell him everything. The tinted windows, the face, the hair, seeing him again the day we went to the acupuncture clinic, Detective Kennedy with the big eyes, the hole in my yard, Connie's hands in his hair, the thing in the paper about the reluctant witness, and me, frozen stiff, not doing anything...until now.

"You were paralyzed with doubts," says Dink the Thinker, thinking out loud.

"I'm going to get closer to him," I say. "Then I'll decide what to do."

"Where do we start?" says Dink.

I like the way he says the word "we."

"We start now," I say. "We're going up to the Hong Kong Beauty Salon — find out what we can about him."

"What about Connie?"

"I don't want her to know — not yet. Not till we're sure…"

Dink whips out his cellular phone from a holster he has tied to his belt at the back. Like Captain James T. Kirk of the Starship *Enterprise* (reruns only), he flips it open and dials 411 and asks for the number of the Hong Kong Beauty Salon and dials the number. It's busy.

"We're going to get you a hair appointment!" says Dink. "Let's go in and show Dad. I've got the Hong Kong on re-dial. I'll whip it out, and bang, we're through to the beauty salon. Then when I'm finished, I'll say, 'Kirk out!' Come on, it'll cheer him up. He's pretty down since he found out we're not going to get blown away by Swift Tuttle!"

We're heading back up Cambridge Street to Somerset. It's snowing harder than ever, and Connie Pan's streetlight looks like a deep hole in space. The walking is tough. They'll plow the main streets tonight but they won't get around to side streets like ours for a couple of days.

The restaurants and stores in Chinatown on Somerset Street look like they're all wearing white hats and scarves and high coat collars made of snow. The red and green neon signs of the shops glow through the snow cover, like they're radioactive, like they're going to melt.

Some of the shopkeepers are out shoveling, but it's no use.

Some are scraping little face holes through the frost on their windows and looking out, making faces.

The Yangtze Restaurant looks like one of those explorer's ships you see in pictures, trapped in the ice in the Arctic Ocean. Jasmine's Sports Bar is below the sidewalk level. You have to go downstairs to go in. But it's filled in with snow.

The sports bar isn't there anymore.

See you in the spring, sports fans!

The delivery guy comes out of Asia Pizza, carrying his pile of pizzas in canvas holders. He's looking around for his delivery car. Is that it, right in front of him, or is that a snowbank?

Dink and I climb up the steps and into the Hong Kong Beauty Salon. It wasn't hard to get an appointment for tonight. A lot of people have canceled.

Eddie Wong, the owner, says Connie's coming in a little later. She's got a couple of specials. And he might have other work for her because his regular hairdresser can't come in because of the snow. You never know on a night like this...

Dink and I sit in the chairs and flip through the magazines — some English, some Chinese, some Vietnamese. On the cover of one of the magazines is a photograph of Ottawa during the Tulip Festival. Sun, green grass, flowers, smiling faces.

I'm wondering if some of the new Canadians came here because they saw this kind of a picture. I guess they were in for a bit of a shock.

How could you ever believe, in your right mind, that a tulip could ever, ever grow in a place like this?

Some of them must think that maybe they got on the wrong plane. Where are the tulips? How come no tulips? Oh, the tulips are under the snow, waiting there, in little bulbs! Honest!

Liar!

A big customer comes in, covered from head to foot in white. She shakes herself like a big dog. She stamps her feet, crashing them on the floor, shaking the Hong Kong Beauty Salon. She whips off her big fur hat and slams it down onto a chair, beating the chair with it. She takes off her leather mitts and whacks them across the counter, slapping the cold out of them. She climbs out of her coat and then shakes the coat, whipping it like she's shaking a dirty mat. She puffs, she sighs, she snorts, grunts, blows her nose, rubs her hands, sighs, shakes her head, sits down.

She looks over at the picture of the tulip on my magazine cover.

"HA!" she says, and slaps her fat knee so hard that it must be stinging.

Another customer is leaving. Eddie is helping him on with his coat. He had a hair wash like I'm going to have. Then dried. Eddie makes a joke about going outside with hair that's not completely dry and frozen brains.

He signs the guy up for an appointment for next week. In the appointment book.

I look at Dink.

Dink sees, too. The appointment book. That's what we want.

We know the date the van driver was last here. It's the day before we made the appointment for Dink's dad at the acupuncture clinic. That date between seven and nine P.M., Connie's hours, when she works during the week.

It's my turn. I don't get Eddie. I get his partner, a woman named Darlene. She knows me a bit and we talk about what a nice person Connie Pan is and what a good worker she is and how some customers want her to do their hair when they come in — just her "special" — nobody else.

Some of them want to write it down in the appointment book, just to be sure. They write down their names, and they write Connie Pan down, too, just to make sure. I want a Connie Pan special…

There's soap in my eyes but I can see enough to see Dink.

He heard.

Now Dink asks Eddie Wong if he can use his phone.

Now he's at the counter, where the appointment book is lying open. Dink flips through the phone book pretending to look up a number. Then he punches up a number and talks into the phone and holds and talks some more and holds, pretending he's on hold.

All the time he's casually looking back through the pages of the appointment book.

Before the big customer gets into Eddie Wong's chair, Eddie takes a Polaroid of her hair from the back and from the front.

She poses pretty for the shots, then whaps herself into the chair.

I ask Darlene how come she didn't take my picture. Darlene says it's just the people who are getting special new hairdos. Eddie likes to show them, after he's done, what they looked like before…

I look over at Dink. He's got a funny look on his face.

I know that look. Something's wrong. What did he see in the appointment book?

In comes Connie Pan.

She's surprised to see me just getting out of the chair.

She's happy to see me and Dink. She thinks it's quite funny, all of a sudden, me, wanting to get my hair washed. She looks a little hurt, too, why she didn't know about it. Maybe she could have done my hair. She's wondering what's going on...

I pay Darlene and we get all our clothes on. Darlene says she hopes she dried my hair completely because we don't want to get frozen brains, do we? We say goodbye to everybody.

Outside, it's snowing even harder. Dink and I stand in the street and talk, our faces close to each other's.

"Did you get the name?"

"Yes, I did," says Dink. "I saw it written twice!"

"Twice?"

"Once, under the date the day before the acupuncture clinic, and again today."

"Today?" I say.

"Tonight. A Connie Pan special. His appointment is fifteen minutes from now!"

We've been outside less than a minute and we're already covered with snow.

XIII

....

It's simple.

As soon as we see him go in the beauty salon to have his hair done, I'll call Detective Kennedy, get the cops over here. We go in, I identify him, they take him away and it's finished.

Once Spud Sweetgrass decides to do something, it gets done in a hurry! That's it, that's all!

We're across the street, waiting in the doorway of the Chinese bookstore, out of the falling snow. There's enough light glowing through the snow on the shops and from the streetlights for us to see people coming in or out of the salon. I have quarters in one mitt and the card with Kennedy's phone number in the other mitt. The phone booth is only eight or ten steps away. We can see it from here, the shape of it, anyway, covered with snow.

We take turns going into the bookstore to get warm. They have magazines in there with naked Chinese girls on the covers.

Dink buys one so the guy won't get mad. "This is not a public library," he always says if you don't buy a magazine right away.

Won't Connie Pan be surprised! Just like on TV. We crash into the place. That's him, grab him!

Then, the last scene. Connie Pan in my arms. "Oh, Spud!" she's saying. "Sh, sh," I'm saying, patting her gentle on the back. "It's all over now...I couldn't tell you..." etc., etc., etc. Then the music...Connie Pan and me, walking off into the snow together, hand in hand. We stop to kiss under the streetlight in front of her house. There's a snowflake on her philtrum...

"His name is Faroni. His first name, just an initial. B," Dink is saying, interrupting my video.

"Probably Bubba or Bruno," I say.

"Address, 206 Cambridge Street."

"He's practically a neighbor of Connie Pan's! What is that place, the apartments? Or no, maybe it's that rooming house."

There's nobody around. Now and then, a car, churning down Somerset through the snow. The plow has been by once but the street is full again. The headlights of the silent car poke through the wall of flakes a bit, then give up and turn to ghosts.

"Are you saying his name to yourself?" says Dink.

"Faroni. Faroni," I repeat.

"No, his first name, too," says Dink.

"We don't know his first name."

"B," says Dink. "B. Faroni. Say it."

"B. Faroni. B. Faroni," I say.

"Yeah," says Dink, laughing. "Beefaroni. Beefaroni! Say it!"

"Beefaroni!" I say. "That's his name? Beefaroni? We used to get that stuff when we were kids when we'd come home from school for lunch."

Everything is funny now. Everything working out. Dink and I, joking around.

"And don't forget his brother, Mac! Mac Aroni!"

"Yeah, the Aroni brothers. Beef, Mac and Rice! The Aroni gang!"

"Detective Marilyn Kennedy arrested a vicious gang of killers today getting their hair done. Mac Aroni getting his washed, Rice Aroni getting rinsed and the prettiest of them all, Beef Aroni, getting his curled!"

"And don't forget that other gang, the Agettis!" I

say, and Dink catches it right away and says, "Oh, you mean, Spag, Alf and Smurf!"

"And there's also Envirogetti!" I say.

"And there's the Atoni brothers," says Dink. Dink is better at this game than I am. He used to work at the IGA bagging groceries. He knows all the products.

"Atoni?" I say. I wish I could get it.

"No, not Atoni," says Dink. "Actually I meant the cousins. You know them. Rig Atoni and his cousin Can. Can Nelloni." Dink is running out of good ones.

I want to keep doing this, but I can't think of any more.

I wish Beefaroni would show up and we could get it over with.

A figure comes down Somerset Street, struggling through the snowdrift on the corner, now dragging to the steps of the beauty salon, taking forever, now up the steps, almost crawling up the snow, and in the door. A little person, not Beefaroni. A kid, maybe. Maybe Connie Pan's mom.

A few minutes go by and the lights of the shop go out. People leave. There's Connie Pan. The figure who went in before is her mom. They fight their way, arm in arm together, down the street. Eddie Wong, the owner, locks up the place.

"What about Tor?" I say to Dink.

"You mean Tor Tellini?" Dink says.

"Yeah," I say. "Tor Tellini. And what about Rav?"

"Yeah," says Dink. "Rav Ioli."

We both stare straight ahead, across the street, through the sheet of falling snow, at the dark windows of the Hong Kong Beauty Salon.

"What about B. Faroni?" says Dink.

"Beefaroni?" I say. "Beefaroni is not going to show up."

It's not hard to catch up to Connie Pan and her mom. Her mom's steps are so short in the deep snow that she doesn't leave footprints. She leaves a narrow, straight little path. We're up to them by the time they are turning down Cambridge. Number 206 is the old apartments near the corner. I don't even look at the place as we shuffle by.

If he's sitting up in his apartment with the window open, holding an extrasensory listening device, he'll hear me telling Connie Pan everything about him.

Connie is already mad at me for going to the salon to get my hair washed without telling her.

When she hears all about Beefaroni and how I saw him in the van driving the shooter, she's more mad at me.

And when she hears about how we talked about

Beef's hair and all that stuff in front of the acupuncture clinic that day and I didn't tell her what was going on, she's even more mad at me.

We're in front of her place now, under the streetlight. I tell her how Dink looked in the appointment book to get Beef's name and tears come to her eyes, she's so mad. Her mom is standing up to her waist in snow, on the front walk to their narrow little house.

"Connie!" she calls. "Connie, come!"

Connie is now as mad as she can get. She can't get any madder and she says she thought we were friends and we shared everything and now she never wants to talk to me again, ever.

Dink is standing at the outside circle of the streetlight. He's holding his right hand up to the light, looking up. He's probably conducting some kind of experiment with crystals and snowflakes and light waves, who knows. He's covered with snow, anyway, like the rest of us.

Connie brushes by him and plows up her front walk. She doesn't want to talk to Dink the Thinker, either. She pushes up her stairs and gets out her key.

Her mom follows her.

Before they go in, her mom stops and turns around.

"Bignose acting weir!" she says. "Go home! You tell you mom, you acting weir!"

Yeah, I know, I'm acting weird. I have been acting weird since the day I saw Beefaroni drive the van so the hit man from Florida could shoot Al Laromano in the back, and I thought I'd protect everybody by dumping what I didn't tell down a hole in the snow. Yes, Mrs. Pan, that is acting weird.

"What are you going to do?" says Dink. The snow on his eyelashes and eyebrows makes him look like a mad scientist who had one of his experiments blow up on him.

"I'm going home to phone Detective Kennedy," I tell him.

"Good idea," says Dink.

The rest of the way home, I feel empty. I'm giving up.

I'll tell my mom everything.

My mom looks peaceful there, reading, the TV on but the sound off.

Part of the way through my story, she puts her book down. Halfway through, she shuts down the TV. When I get to the part where I saw Beefaroni on the street, she comes over and hugs me. By the end, I don't feel empty anymore.

She sits with me while I call Detective Kennedy. I get her on the answering machine.

I hang up.

"Call again, and leave your name and number this time," Mom says, very gently.

I call and do that.

I hang up and wait.

My mom has sadness in her eyes. I don't blame her. It must feel awful when your only kid makes a complete fool of himself.

My mom takes my hand.

"You're just like your father. Brave. Bravery involves risks. Sometimes bravery ends in heroism. Sometimes in foolishness. Your father was on the side of right when he caused the uproar at the paper mill over the pollution. He was right. But he was fired…"

There's a long pause. A long wait. There's more she wants to say. All of a sudden, I'm tired. It was very cold out there, waiting, across from the beauty salon…being a fool.

Here comes more from my mom. Her voice is so soothing. I love the way she loves me…

"Did you think that there might be a Polaroid of this character with the fancy hair? Did they take a shot of him — a snapshot of him before Connie did his hair the last time…?"

I'm wide awake! What did she say?

A photograph! Why didn't I think of that! Beefaroni's photo! What an idiot I am! Dink didn't even think of it. It took my mom to see that…to figure that! A photo of the Beef!

"Tell your Detective Kennedy's big blue eyes about a possible photo of this creep. She's going to love that!"

My mom goes to get ready for bed and I lie down on the couch by the phone, waiting for Detective Marilyn Kennedy to call.

Everything is so quiet. The snow muffles everything, even in the house. It feels so good to have it over with. Tomorrow, when it stops snowing, I'll go out and open the hole. Some people might think that's stupid, but the old story says if you don't release the facts once they are no longer secret, the hole will never work for you ever again.

Then, after it's open, invite everybody up for a party, like we used to when my father was alive. The house full of people…laughing and singing…

The phone's ringing and I answer it. It's B. Faroni. I put him on the speaker phone. He wants to talk to my mom. My mom comes out of the bedroom. She's all dressed up. Going out to a party. B. Faroni is saying his hair is just the way she likes it and he'll be here in a minute. My mom gets her coat on and a fur hat. B. Faroni is at the door. There's a big pile of snow on top of his new hair. A conehead. My mom says he looks lovely. They begin to dance around the room. The orchestra is playing a big number. My father is the leader of the band. He plays "Hanging Gardens" on his trombone, a song that he wrote and was a big hit. The last note he plays on his trombone is so long and strong, the wind from it blows the snow off B. Faroni's head and straightens out his hairdo. My mom is being blown away in the blizzard and I'm grabbing her to keep her from being blown away. I have her by the clothes but her clothes are ripping. B. Faroni's in slow motion...he's got a rifle sticking out of a brown van...his face is close to the tinted window...the trombone is ringing.

"Telephone, Johnnie! Johnnie! Get the phone!" My mother is calling from her bedroom.

Half asleep. I'm sitting up on the couch, puffing and sweating. There's the sound of faraway fire reels.

I say hello into the phone.

It's Connie Pan. She's not mad at me anymore. She's excited. She's saying there's a picture of him. They took his picture the last time she did his hair. It's in the counter drawer in the beauty salon, underneath where the appointment book is. She's talking fast.

"I have his picture, Spud! The Polaroid! We can give it to the police. They can put it in the newspaper. Then everybody in Ottawa is a witness!"

I ask if she has a key to get in. She has. I ask if she

can go out right now, even though it's late. Her mother's asleep. She can. I tell her I'll see her under her streetlight in ten minutes.

I phone Detective Marilyn Kennedy again.

Still the answering machine.

I leave my message again.

Phone Spud Sweetgrass. Urgent.

I get dressed and go out.

I close the door gentle, not to wake my great mom.

XIV

....

It's stopped snowing!

The map from my door to Connie Pan's is this: out my door onto Rochester Street, immediate right onto Anderson for one block, left onto Booth for a bit, right on Eccles for two blocks, left up Cambridge to the Pans' narrow house and Connie's door.

I say it's a map because, right now, at two A.M., I have to cut a trail, a new trail, through the new snow from my door to Connie's. I'm a map-maker, a trail-blazer.

She's not mad at me anymore. She's part of it now. The way it should have been from the start. My partner. No more secrets.

It's stopped snowing. The city is beautiful. The

temperature seems warm. It's only minus 28 on my veranda thermometer. Almost not dangerous.

I feel excited.

Is that the sound of fire alarms, or was that in my dream?

The new snow is poured over everything like whipped cream. Everything available is loaded with snow, with the heavy thick cream, sagging with the beautiful weight. Every tiny twig, of every stem, of every bough, of every branch of every tree, is loaded with every flake that it can take! I look back down Anderson at the path I've made. My path and my path only.

It's exciting, but as I turn onto Booth Street, I feel there's something missing. There's a gap somewhere. Up Eccles Street, past Dink the Thinker's, I can still feel that there's something not there that should be there...

As I plunge around the corner onto Cambridge Street and look up towards Somerset, the streetlights there seem to have an extra glow now that the snow has stopped. It's like the lights are waiting for a big show to start. A big song with lots of people dancing.

Connie Pan is waiting out in front of her house. The fur of her hood makes a round frame for her face. She reminds me of an old photograph on a wall of somebody's great-grandmother when she was young and beautiful.

When I tell her how sorry I am, she says a short sentence that she has ready. I can tell she planned it, practiced it.

"Don't protect me, Spud. Include me."

Under the streetlight, she shows me a key. The key to the Hong Kong Beauty Salon, and to Beefaroni's photograph, which we'll hand over to Detective Marilyn Kennedy, who will give it to the newspapers, and then, Connie Pan is right, everybody in the Ottawa Valley will know what Mr. Beefaroni looks like! Not just us!

There's a lot of action up on Somerset Street. As we get closer, it gets more like chaos. There's sirens, flashing lights, sounds of shouting, a glow in the sky.

A fire! Near the Hong Kong Beauty Salon! As we get closer, we can't believe what we see.

It's the Hong Kong Beauty Salon that's on fire!

There's fire trucks, ambulances, police cars, plows, cars everywhere, pointing in every direction. There are three ladders against the walls and firemen walking in and out of the smoke on the roof. There are two hoses pumping water into the black smoke.

There's ice everywhere. Walls of colored ice flowing down off the roof and plunging out the windows. A river of ice gushes out the front door and spills down the steps. The big window that you could look in and see the people in the chairs getting their hair done is gone and yellow ice is oozing out of the gap like pus.

Connie and I both see at once.

The counter where the appointment book was kept is a twisted, black wreck.

And the drawers, where Beefaroni's picture should have been?

They don't exist anymore.

The Polaroid is burnt up.

Holding hands, Connie and I pick our way over frozen hoses and equipment, past the roaring pumper truck, to the officer in the police car. His door is open and we can hear his radio growling.

We explain to him that we are witnesses and could he call Detective Marilyn Kennedy to see if she's trying to find me.

We watch the firemen struggle with the ice and snow. The Hong Kong Beauty Salon is toasted. The shops on each side are saved. There's Eddie Wong, the owner, just got here. He's going around like a crazy man. He's swearing away in English and Chinese. He walks right by Connie, doesn't even see her. He's lost his mind. He's tearing his clothes, he's beating his hat against the side of one of the fire trucks. He's throwing his mitts on the ground, he's jumping on his mitts and his hat, grinding them into the filthy snow.

"Poor, poor Eddie," says Connie Pan. "His whole life is doing hair…"

The cop in the car calls out, "Detective Kennedy's on her way!"

Along comes Dink the Thinker. He's half asleep. Behind him, his dad. He's not half asleep. Dink's dad doesn't sleep much. Dink's dad has black circles under the black circles under his eyes. Connie and Dink talk about apologizing. They're friends again. Dink says he has an idea about maybe the Hong Kong Beauty Salon had a photo of Beefaroni…

Go back to bed, Dink. We're way ahead of you!

Dink's dad says he hopes that this fire wasn't caused by a cigarette smoker.

"We've got a bad enough reputation as it is," he says. He's trying to smoke with mitts on. His cigarette is burning the wool of his smoking mitt.

A police car makes one whoop sound.

It's Detective Kennedy, rolling down her window.

"Get in," she says.

We do.

I introduce Connie to her.

"She's a witness I didn't mention to you."

"What else didn't you mention?"

I tell her everything, describe everything. Connie tells her everything, describes Beefaroni. Tells how I didn't let her in on it until now, trying to protect her.

"Men, eh?" Detective Marilyn Kennedy says to Connie Pan, and winks one of her large blue eyes at both of us.

A tall, handsome fireman talks private to Detective Kennedy.

She knows him. Calls him Andy.

Then Connie tells her something that makes her hit her radio and get pretty excited.

She tells her Beefaroni's address.

We hear fireman Andy talk about chemicals. Obvious. Arson.

Connie and I look at each other.

Just what we were thinking.

Beefaroni, breaks in, looks all over, can't find his picture. He thinks it must be there somewhere so he sets fire to the place. That's what happened. Beefaroni destroying his identity.

Connie and me and Dink and his dad walk down Cambridge and watch the two police cars park right in the middle of the road in front of number 206. The cops go in. We stand around. They're not going to find him. He's not there. Didn't think he would be.

Detective Kennedy talks to the supervisor of Beefaroni's building.

He's got on a big parka and boots, but you can tell he just put them on over his pajamas. He's telling the cops that Beefaroni was never around much.

"Was only here for three months. Never around much. Fancy dresser. Great hair. Loved his hair!"

The superintendent's own hair is sticking out under his hat like dried leaves. He hasn't got great hair. And his teeth are clicking together. He's cold. The minus 28 is running up under his pajamas.

Connie Pan and me, we're smiling.

Detective Kennedy asks us if we'll help the police artist draw a picture of Beefaroni. She'll call us soon to make an appointment with the artist.

"This is the weekend so we'll have to make arrangements. Won't be able to get it in the paper till Monday or Tuesday…"

Time to go home. It's over. They'll catch the Beef eventually. Just a matter of time…

Back down to Connie's narrow house. The house is now wearing a very heavy white hood. It looks like a skinny nun with sad eyes for windows.

Connie has no house key. She pulls out of her pocket the key to the Hong Kong Beauty Salon. We look at it in the light of Connie's streetlight. Wrong key.

Connie sadly drops the key into the snow, and it disappears just like it would if she'd dropped it into the ocean. Don't need that key anymore.

She decides not to get her mother out of bed to let her in. Too much fuss.

I'm glad of this. I don't feel like getting insulted by Mrs. Pan. Connie decides she's going to go in the back shed window. She crawled in there once before when she forgot her key, but not in the winter.

The snow clouds are gone. There's a moon up there and some stars.

We go around the back of her house in snow up to our waists. The window she's going in is too high to reach. She says she used a ladder last time, the ladder that is leaning up against the old garage. There's the old garage, but where's the ladder?

On our hands and knees we dig for the ladder. We find the first five rungs of it. The next five rungs are deep into a few layers of crust, the same layers as you might come across while digging a hole to say a secret into.

I wrench the ladder back and forward till it loosens up. We're making quite a bit of noise. Putting our shoulders under the rungs, we dislodge it from the grip of all the snow that came down so far this year, on what is now maybe the planet's newest coldest capital city.

Under the window against the wall of the shed, there's a wooden bench down there somewhere. We shove the ladder down into the snow until it stops somewhere over where the bench should be.

The moon helps by shining his light on our work.

I test the ladder with my weight, and it sinks a little more and then holds.

Connie climbs up the ladder and pushes in the window. It's on hinges and it isn't locked but it's stuck, and she has to whap the frame a couple of times.

More noise.

The window opens and she leans in and hooks it to the ceiling inside. She crawls through and disappears but then appears again immediately. She's kneeling on a cupboard in there. She's resting out the window on her arms. The moon is reflecting, showing her face framed in fur.

She leans her cheek on her mitt.

Oh, I wish I was the mitt on that hand!

She doesn't seem to want to go in.

"I promise I won't leave you out again," I whisper as loud as I can. "From now on, we share!"

"Promise?"

"I swear."

"You swear by what?"

"I swear by…the moon…"

"The moon changes…many times."

This is quite a romantic conversation we're having. I'm getting a little bit hoarse from whispering so loud.

"The moon only looks like it's changing. Actually it's the same old moon all the time." This is starting to get pretty complicated.

From inside the house somewhere there comes the sound of Connie Pan's mom.

"Connie. Connie…" Then some Chinese words meaning where are you, what are you doing up, why aren't you in bed.

"I have to go…" says Connie.

"Goodnight, Connie," I say, looking up.

"This ladder, will it hold your weight, Spud?" asks Connie.

Mrs. Pan is yelling long sentences in Chinese.

I climb a few rungs until my face is even with Connie's.

She kisses me on the lips.

She taps me on the nose.

"Goodnight, Bignose," says Connie.

She laughs like a quiet whispering bell.

She shuts the window.

I fall backwards off the ladder into the soft snow.

On my back I imagine I'm in a camera close-up. Now the camera is fading back, up. Now you can see the roof of Connie Pan's narrow house, you can see me lying in the yard in the snow, arms out, legs apart. Now you see the whole of Chinatown, now I'm only a small X, now the whole city, now the whole winter night, Canada from space, the planet Earth from the moon, now only a speck in space and time…

On my way home, down Anderson, I'm getting the funny feeling I had before. The feeling of something missing…a gap…something is there because it's not there…

But the gap goes away. It is filled now with Connie Pan's whispering laugh, the feel of our lips together, the feel of having no weight, falling out of the sky into her backyard snow, soft falling like an angel, through the perfect and beautiful and frozen air of her backyard, falling off her beautiful ladder, seeing her disappear into her perfect window, lying in the cold, warm snow like a perfect speck in the universe…

XV

··

After I make breakfast I'm going over to Connie Pan's to help her get ready for her E.S.L. skating party on the Rideau Canal, the world's longest skating rink.

Connie also wants me to help her do a snow sculpture for Ottawa Tech at the snow sculpture contest on Dow's Lake. She wants to make a statue of a creature made from the funny names of places she found in her Canadian geography book.

Here's what she wants to make. The creature will have the body of a mermaid, because of a place called Mermaid, in Prince Edward Island. It will be holding a blunt pen because of Blunt Pen, N.W.T. It will have its rear end painted gold for Gold Bottom, Yukon. It will have balls at the back for Rear Balls, Nova Scotia.

It will have three arms for Three Arms, Newfoundland; five fingers for Five Fingers, New Brunswick; an ox's tongue for Ox Tongue, Ontario; the tail of a bird for Bird Tail, Manitoba; a flat head for Flat Head, British Columbia; a hat shaped like a bottle of Tylenol for Medicine Hat, Alberta; the jaw of a moose for Moose Jaw, Saskatchewan. And it will be laughing because of the Quebec town which is called St. Louis du HA! HA!

I don't know how we're going to make this out of snow, but that's her plan. She's going to call it "Funny Canada."

Someday Connie Pan will be famous.

The statue will be hard to do, but getting ready for the party on the world's longest skating rink will be easy. Dow's Lake is the beginning of the rink. You skate from there about eight kilometers all the way down the Rideau Canal to the Parliament Buildings, where the canal empties into the mighty Ottawa River. Right near my all-time favorite statue, the statue of Samuel de Champlain, the first of all the new Canadians.

Everybody in Canada, except the Abos (they were already here), comes from somewhere else. Champlain was the first new Canadian. If he showed up now, almost four hundred years later, he could come skating with Connie Pan's E.S.L. group. And, once he got his skates on, Connie would pin the piece of cloth that she printed with his name and country on it to the back of his coat. "Sam Champlain, France," it would say.

It seems funny, Sam Champlain coming up the Ottawa River and stopping right near where his statue is now because he was actually looking for China.

If he came now, all he'd have to do is park his canoe down below the Chateau Laurier there, walk up Parliament Hill, go over to Ottawa Tech, go up another hill along Bronson Avenue and he'd be right on Somerset Street in Chinatown. That would be a nice surprise for him! He could write a letter back to the king of France and tell him he found China on a street called Somerset.

I'll make my mom's favorite breakfast before I go over to Connie's. It's early yet. Nobody's up. I make the breakfast my dad used to make for us. It's fried potato cakes with garlic. Because he's not here, I cut the recipe in half for just my mom and me.

Cook three slices of bacon in the microwave until they're done too much. Smash them up in tiny pieces. Boil two big potatoes with lots of garlic until the potatoes are almost done. Peel and mash the potatoes and mix in three handfuls of flour, two eggs, some nutmeg, half a chopped-up onion, about three big blobs of cottage cheese, the smashed-up bacon, some salt and pepper. Mix it with your hands until it's like a sloppy softball. Shape into two large pancakes. Fry the cakes in a little bit of sizzling hot olive oil.

Put the two potato cakes on hot plates on a big tray with orange juice, coffee and a jar of homemade raspberry jam with my father's handwriting on the label. It's the last jar of a batch he made two years ago.

My mom's awake. She's sitting up in bed reading. She acts surprised but I know she knows that this is coming. She's been listening and smelling.

While we eat, she looks at me like I'm some kind of a movie star or something.

The perfect son. Makes his mother her favorite breakfast and brings it to her in bed on Saturday morning.

I do some toast for the raspberry jam and bring it in just in time. And another coffee.

"They didn't catch your crook with the ridiculous name yet," my mom says. She puts my father's raspberry jam on her toast so careful, like it is melted gold.

"This Beefaroni person, does he have a brother named Mac?" my mom says, keeping her face straight like she always does when she makes a joke.

"Yeah," I say. "Dink and I went through all the names...the Agetti brothers, Spag and Alf..." My mom smiles.

We have a little more jam.

"Those potato cakes were the best you've ever made," my mom says, getting serious. Then she starts to sound like Connie Pan. "You'll share with me when you can…the things you're doing…"

I nod. I'll try.

All I can hear is toast crunching.

"This is the last of the jam," I say, changing the subject.

"I know," she says, sadness in her voice.

More toast crunching.

"Good, in a way," she says. "Got to let go. We'll keep the label on the jar…I always loved his handwriting…"

I feel pain.

"We're going to stop leaving his chair empty over there at the Village Inn. Enough is enough…"

While my mom gets ready to go out, I check the temperature and do the dishes.

The perfect son.

It's minus 36. The coldest day yet. The wind chill makes it close to minus 50. On days like this, Inuit living in the Arctic don't even go out. They stay in and sleep like sensible people. My mom and I are both going out. She's going to work on the guy under the bed and some other projects at the cultural center and

I'm going to Connie's. We laugh about all the clothes we have to put on to go out into the cold.

Outside the narrow house of Connie Pan there's a taxi parked along the snowbank. The bank is almost as high as the taxi. Mr. Pan and the driver have a huge box wedged halfway into the back of the taxi. The trunk is already packed with cases and boxes and won't shut. There are trunks and suitcases half buried in the snowbank. Is Mr. Pan just getting here or is he just leaving? You can't tell. You never know.

At Connie's, I help work on the name cloths to pin on the backs of the E.S.L. skaters. While I'm cutting out the cloth I'm hoping that she doesn't want to talk about the Funny Canada sculpture.

"What about the Funny Canada sculpture," says Connie. "When do we start to make it?"

"Any time you want," I say.

"We will do these names first," she says.

We have the list of names of the E.S.L. group. Connie Pan has a world globe and she has little tags pinned on the globe showing where each kid comes from. They all come from the top half of the world. Not one of the eighteen new Canadians comes from below the equator.

Seven who come from closest to the equator come from the Philippines and Vietnam. Since they come from the hottest places, they probably haven't got very many rinks, so they might not be able to skate very well. But you never know.

Six who come from farthest away from the equator like Russia, Hungary, Ukraine, Estonia and Romania are probably good skaters. They have lots of ice to skate on there. But you never know. The five people from China, Lebanon, India and Iran are probably in-between skaters, but, you never know. Especially about skating.

You ask some people, can they skate. They say yes, they're really good skaters. You go skating with them, they can't even stand up.

You ask some other people, can they skate. They say just average. You go skating with them, they wind up going around like Elvis Stojko!

Connie decides to divide the new Canadians into groups of three. Each group will have a captain, who is probably a good skater, from the north, but you never know.

Here are the teams:

I   Alexander Baraev – Russia (Captain)
     Roberto Adriano – Philippines
     Jose Rafael Aguasin – Philippines

We're on the floor working on the cloth signs.

In comes Mrs. Pan. She looks at me one way, walks around the other side, looks at me again, walks back, looks at me again, walks back, looks me over again.

"Good morning, Bignose! Not acting weir today?"

"Good morning, Mrs. Pan. No, not acting weir today. Acting weir all finished," I say. I'm trying not to imitate her, but it's hard.

I'm on my knees on the floor. Mrs. Pan is standing in front of me. We are face to face. We are the same height. Connie is standing behind Mrs. Pan, looking at me.

"Big mess in yard last night," Mrs. Pan says. "Ladder moved. Snow all broken. Many feet stepping…"

Connie Pan is behind her, watching me, having lots of fun.

"You know what happen to yard, Bignose?"

"No, I don't, Mrs. Pan," I say, very polite.

"Who could be…?" says Mrs. Pan. "Move ladder, run all around!"

"Aliens, maybe?" I say. "People from outer space? Visitors from other planet?"

"Ya," says Mrs. Pan. "Maybe visitors from *this* planet, maybe, eh? This planet!"

Behind her, Connie Pan, making faces.

I go back to cutting the pieces of cloth on the floor. Mrs. Pan puts on about seven coats and goes outside to help her husband get the taxi packed so he can get to the airport.

The phone rings. Connie answers.

It's for me. It's my mom, calling from the cultural center.

Detective Kennedy called.

She wants me to call her right away at the police station.

It's important.

XVI

On Saturday afternoon, Connie Pan and me are at the police station standing beside Detective Kennedy and the computer artist.

The face of Beefaroni is being drawn on the screen by the computer artist.

Make his face more square. Put his eyes wider apart. Make his lips look like they're carved out of wood. Draw a little mustache, like with a pencil. Now, rub it out. Make the eyebrows thicker. Join them up in the middle. Now, his eyes are smaller. And his forehead comes out more.

His hair, make it bigger. More curly. No, wavy. Higher. Fatter hair. A little longer. Sideburns bushier. Big waves.

"Hey, this is great hair!" says the computer artist.

Detective Kennedy takes us into her office.

"We have certain phones tapped and we know that your friend Faroni has called these people several times looking for money to get out of town with. We don't know where he's called from. We've heard them say this about Faroni: 'He's got the witness in his house.' It's been said a couple of times. 'He's got the witness in his house.' We've been back, of course, to where he was living and he's long gone from there." Detective Kennedy pauses, waiting…letting it sink in like she likes to do…

"I called you right away, you being the witnesses," says Detective Kennedy. She's trying to drown Connie and me in her eyes.

"What do you think they mean?" she says. "He's got the witness in his house?"

Connie looks at me. Am I hiding something again, she seems to be saying.

"I hate this Beefaroni!" she says. Detective Kennedy smiles.

I'm thinking.

I'm thinking about it all Saturday night down at Dow's Lake while Connie and Dink and I try to build Connie's sculpture, "Funny Canada." Nothing is working and Connie's getting frustrated. The mermaid body doesn't look anything like a mermaid and forget about trying to put fish scales on it. And the tail doesn't look like a bird's tail. It looks like a beaver's tail. The head is flat, that's easy, but the medicine bottle is impossible. And the jaw of a moose? Forget it. A moose nose would be easier. We try to spray-paint the bottom in gold but it doesn't make sense. An ox tongue? Can't do it. St. Louis du HA! HA! Doesn't work. Hardly any of it works. Three arms and five fingers are OK. But a blunt pen? Forget it. It looks like a cigar. The rear balls we don't even try.

Next to us, another group is doing Bart Simpson. And it's pretty good. They'll probably win. It's not Canadian but nobody seems to care about that.

A little farther down, Roddy and Fabio are building a huge ice-penis.

Connie gets disgusted and we give up and go home. It's too cold, anyway.

On Sunday I help Connie finish the signs for the E.S.L. skating party.

We make one more sign saying "Follow Me!" Connie is going to wear it on her back, once she gets the teams organized. It's the best sign of all. It's really flashy and is done with fluorescent spray.

We go over to Dink the Thinker's to make the final plans for skating on the world's longest skating rink.

Dink's dad was at a hypnotist yesterday. This is the last, he's saying. He's tried everything to quit the weed. He's tried nicotine gum. It gave him toothaches. Nicotine patches. They kept him awake at night. He tried making his apartment a non-smoking area with posters all over. He even had a big blow-up poster of a guy named Wayne McLaren who was that cowboy, the Marlboro Man, in all the cigarette ads. (He died of lung cancer.) Didn't work.

He tried breathing deeply, eating celery, laser therapy, behavior modification, habit substitution, acupuncture and now, hypnosis. He tells us about what happened at the hypnotist's office.

"I was in a group in his office. We were all sitting in a row. He was in his office chair on wheels. He kept pouring water in water glasses and drinking out of them and lining them up on his desk and talking about when we were kids. Then he'd wheel over on his office chair and speak to each one of us individually about when we were kids, before we started to smoke, and taking sips of all these glasses of water. I started thinking about the girl in grade two during the Remembrance Day ceremony peeing on the stage. I remembered her name and everything! Imagine! I can remember her name but I can't remember the name of my best friend in grade two! You always remember the people's names who did embarrassing things when you were a kid but you can never remember the name of the kid who came first in the class or the kid who got killed by the streetcar! But I remember the name of the kid who belched during grace at the birthday party! This is what I was doing at the hypnosis session. I couldn't stop myself! I don't know if it was the water or what! I could remember the name of the kid who blew snot all over the birthday candles. I could name you the kid who spit in his chocolate milk. And the kid whose balls fell out during the gymnastics show! I can't tell you the name of the kid who saved me from drowning one time, but I can tell you the name of the kid who farted in church, who puked on the bus! I don't remember the name of the teacher who taught me how to swim but I'll never forget the kid's name who pooped the big log in the pool that day!"

Dink's dad's got three cigarettes going at once while he's telling us this. Connie Pan and I, we're laughing so hard, we're crying.

"He's smoking worse than ever," says Dink. "The hypnosis just made him worse."

Dink's dad goes in the other room and turns on the TV.

We get down to work.

Our plan for the skating party is this.

We'll skate from Dow's Lake to the other end. It's the opening of Winterlude, so the crowd will be huge. The paper says there will be 100,000 people there.

It's a long way to skate, so the E.S.L. skaters will be hungry when they get there. If they get there. You never know.

Stuff can happen. You can break a skate lace. Get too tired. Fall and sprain something. Freeze your face.

Connie Pan wants to order hot beavertails for everybody. A beavertail is a big, flat, delicious chunk of fried dough filled with jam or garlic cheese or whatever you want.

Beavertails take a while to make and there'll be line-ups so Connie wants us to phone ahead, when we're about three-quarters of the way there, so the beavertails will be ready.

We'll use Dink's cellular.

Dink will wait by the pay phone in the warm Arts Center restaurant to get the call. Then he will get in line and order all the beavertails.

Dink writes the whole scheme up in his scientific writing style on his computer: *Obtain specific orders for beavertails from each skater. Post beavertail contact man next to public phone in Arts Center. Phone contact man at 3/4 way through course...*

I take Dink's cellular and go home.

I grab a quick supper and check the temperature. Pretty good. It's only minus 25. And no wind chill. A clear night. Perfect for skating. My mom is going. Mrs. Pan. Even Dink's dad. Everybody's going. Down to Dow's Lake. Not far from my place.

I get dressed warm but not too heavy. It's half past six. I sling my skates over my shoulder, shout at Mom I'll see her later, stick the cellular phone in my side pocket and button the flap, go down the back stairs into my yard.

It doesn't look like there ever was a hole dug in the snow here.

It's a beautiful night. Sky clear, lights on, winter twinkling, snow in my yard piled around like all the shaving cream in the world.

What Detective Kennedy heard over the phone, "He's got the witness in his house," is still stuck in my head. Stuck there like a piece of ice on a wool mitt.

I go out the brown doors of my yard. The street is packed with hard smooth snow.

I'm standing exactly where I stood when it all started. When I became the witness.

But, wait a minute!

Something's missing.

Where's the laneway man?

XVII

....

That's what was missing!

After the dream I had about Beefaroni dancing with my mom and then when I walked over to Connie's and then the fire.

Something was missing.

And then, the gap, when I walked home after I fell off Connie's ladder — the thing that was wrong.

And there it is right down the street. The laneway man's laneway is not shoveled. It's full to the brim with snow!

Where is he?

Could it be?

Maybe I'm not the witness, after all.

It's the laneway man.

Beefaroni thinks the laneway man is the witness!

A taxi pulls up in front of the laneway man's house. I move closer. There's somebody coming down the plugged laneway. He's up to his knees in the snow. He's carrying skates.

The man reaches the taxi, yanks open the back door. The light from inside shows his face. He's got a big fur hat on but I can still see enough in the quick light.

It's him.

It's Beefaroni!

"Dow's Lake!" he says to the driver and gets in and slams the door.

XVIII

....

The taxi starts to pull away. I run up and grab the back bumper and get into a crouch.

The hard-packed snow is perfect.

Let's ride!

The whole time I'm hanging onto the bumper of the taxi, a video is rolling on all the screens in my head. No matter where I look, the same show is playing.

It's the Beefaroni show.

Beefaroni, checks out his tinted window, looks at brown doors, nobody there, pulls out and starts away. And there, leaning on his shovel, is the laneway man. Nobody else around. Beefaroni thinks, did this guy see or didn't he? He looks like he's only interested in shoveling but maybe he saw. Beefaroni decides to wait.

Maybe he saw, maybe he didn't. But then, in the paper, it says "reluctant witness"! Beefaroni thinks it must be him, goes to his house, breaks in...I can't see any more...it's too awful.

I'm in a crouch, hanging onto the bumper. Rochester Street is perfect for sliding. No other time of the year could I do this. All other times, the salt would have cleared the street to the pavement. Now, my boots glide along the hard surface.

At the second red light at Gladstone, I pull out Dink's cellular and call Detective Kennedy. It's her machine.

I leave a message about the laneway man and that Beefaroni's heading for Dow's Lake and I'm following.

There are hundreds of people walking with skates over their shoulders. Everybody heading for the world's longest skating rink.

The taxi turns down a side street and stops at the light at Preston. I call Dink's house but he's already left.

There's a huge traffic pile-up. Everybody's going skating.

The taxi creeps onto Preston Street and suddenly I'm on my face!

Pavement! This is a main street. This street is always black. Horns are honking. I get up and start to jog. My mitts are stuck to the bumper of the taxi. I get to

Carling and catch up to the cab at the red light there. The cars are moving slow. I pull my mitts off the bumper and walk while I watch the taxi pull into the parking area at Dow's Lake.

There's a swarm of people here. I watch the big fur hat on Beefaroni's head get out of the cab and move through the crowd. He heads over towards the first change shack and goes in. There's skating music playing over speakers and people are taking off on their skates across the lake.

Winterlude is beginning.

There are line-ups all over for hot dogs and coffee and hot chocolate. There are sleighs with bells on them and old people strapped to toboggans being towed by skaters. There are babies tied to skaters' backs and lovers taking off, holding hands. There are people who can skate like the wind and people who can hardly stand up. There are families getting organized, groups making plans, kids crying, people fixing skates, boys helping girls tighten their skates, girls fixing boys' scarves, show-offs buzzing in and out, people doing figures, people standing there helpless, people going the wrong way, people skating on their ankles, people crawling, people lying on their backs, people skating off into the dark with their hands behind their backs, couples dancing on skates, people skating in threes and fours arm in arm, people tied together with rope, people helping other people who look like they're going to die, people singing, laughing, crying, kissing, puffing, blowing, sniffing, complaining, cheering, calling, teasing, waving banners, dragging streamers, carrying sparklers, flashing flashlights, waving fluorescent mitts. Skate blades are gleaming in the colored lights.

I go into the change shack. It's jammed with people. Beefaroni's in the corner on the edge of a bench taking off his boots. He's putting on his skates. I get a spot on another bench where I can keep an eye on him through the crowd.

In comes Connie Pan with a couple of her E.S.L. skaters. She starts handing out their name cloths and helping them put on their skates. She sees me and comes over. She starts talking about getting the beavertail orders written down.

"I want to share something with you," I say to her, without looking at her. I won't take my eyes off Beefaroni. "Beefaroni's sitting right over there. Don't look over. I've called Kennedy. They're coming. Don't look at him. Keep getting everybody ready…"

"I will share something with you," says Connie Pan, her eyes wide with excitement. She pulls out the Polaroid of Beefaroni from her jacket.

"Eddie Wong had it in his pocket the whole time.

He was going to make a before-and-after poster of some of the customers!" Now Connie's eyes narrow. So that's why he burned down the beauty parlor. He couldn't find the photo!

She looks slyly over at Beef.

Beefaroni has caused us to fight. He burned down the place where she works. Now, is this skating party going to be ruined, too?

Connie hates Beefaroni. You can tell by the way she side-spies him out of the corners of her eyes.

More E.S.L.ers come in. Connie is getting them together. Getting their skates on, their name cloths pinned on. She's talking to the captains. Things aren't the way we thought they'd be. One of the Russians says now he's never skated before. The guy from the Philippines, it turns out, has won some skating medals. You never know. The Estonian, who said he often skated, turns out he's often skated alright, but only on roller skates! You never know.

And, Fatima, the girl from India, when Connie asked her if she could skate, she just shrugged her shoulders. Well, now she's already out on the ice doing triple axels! You never know.

Two men in overcoats and no skates come into the change shack and go over and stand over Beefaroni. He's finishing lacing up his skates.

They give him a brown envelope.

There's sweat running down his face. It's coming from underneath his big fur hat.

The two men in overcoats leave.

Beefaroni stands up, puts the envelope in his inside coat pocket, pulls on his gloves and heads towards the door. His boots are hanging around his neck. He's leaving. He's got the money. He's going to skate off and escape. Where are the cops?

I look over at Connie Pan.

She looks at me. Then she looks at him. She calls out to her E.S.L. party.

"Everybody ready?" she shouts.

Then she goes over to Beefaroni just as he gets to the door. She slaps him on the back. I can't believe what I'm seeing!

"Hi, Mr. Faroni! 'Member me? Your hairdresser! How the hell are you!"

I've never heard Connie Pan talk like this before. Saying "hell" like that.

"I have not seen you for a while," says Connie, laughing. "You miss your appointment!"

She's still got her hand on his back, patting his back, as she's talking, like a friend.

"But then, too bad, beauty parlor burned down! Can't fix your hair no more! HA! HA! HA!"

I'm hypnotized by what Connie is doing. She's sounding like her mother. She's laughing away and talking like Beef's her very best friend.

Beef's looking straight ahead at the door. He's trying not to attract any attention. But he's the center of attention here in the shack.

Connie's hand is still on his back. What's she doing? She's pinning the "Follow Me!" sign on his back!

She's closing the big safety pin with her fingers, pinning the sign on his coat, patting at the same time. There, the sign is on. Pat some more. Pat the sign. Some of the E.S.L. skaters are smiling. It doesn't matter what country you're from on this planet, pinning a sign on somebody's back when they don't know it is funny.

Some of the E.S.L. skaters are laughing now. Connie Pan is saying goodbye to her friend, Beefaroni.

"Goodbye, Mr. Faroni. Have a pleasant skate this evening. Maybe see you around some time!"

One more slap on the back. One for the road.

Beefaroni goes out.

"Let's go!" cries Connie Pan. "Follow me!" she shouts, pointing at Beef's back.

All the E.S.L. skaters are laughing now. This is going to be a good party.

Just follow the guy in the funny hat with the fluorescent sign on his back!

Everybody piles out and takes off after Beefaroni.

Lucky for us, Beefaroni is not a very good skater. He can stand up OK and move along, but he has no style and he's slow. When you have no style, you use a lot of energy skating and you get tired easy. Then your style gets even worse.

At the other side of Dow's Lake we move into the narrow canal.

There are thousands of people along Colonel By Drive, leaning over the railings watching the skaters, cheering and laughing.

A lot of people see the "Follow Me!" sign and point and laugh. You can tell when somebody doesn't know he's wearing a sign on his back. You can tell by the way he acts.

I call Detective Kennedy again. I'm wondering did Captain Kirk ever use his communicator while he was on skates? They switch me to Kennedy's car phone.

She answers. She just got to Dow's Lake.

"You missed him," I say.

"Where the hell are you, Sweetgrass!" says Detective Kennedy. She's starting to sound like Connie Pan.

"We just went under Bronson Bridge," I tell her.

"We're about ten minutes from the Bank Street Bridge. Beef's not that great a skater!"

"How will we see you? There's thousands of people!" she says.

"You'll see us, all right," I say. "Beef's sort of the center of attention! He glows in the dark!" I press End.

This is fun.

We skate under the Bank Street Bridge. It is high above us. Hundreds of people are lined up on both sides of the bridge. They're shouting down at the skaters.

They're dropping powdery snow down on us.

The snow is shining in the lights floating down on us. It glitters in the lights against the black sky.

We shout back at the people. Laughing and shouting. The people's voices echo under the bridge. Everybody's having fun.

Except Mr. Faroni. He's working so hard, he hasn't got time to have any fun.

His skating style is rotten.

First of all, he pumps his arms too much. He pumps his arms about five times to take only one step.

He skates like two different people. The top half of B. Faroni is acting like he's skating at about the speed of light. It's acting like he's on a big breakaway with the puck in the last few seconds of a one-one tie in the seventh game of the Stanley Cup final.

But the bottom half of Beefaroni couldn't beat a turtle in a race. It is acting like a kid on double runners for the first time in his life.

But one thing we can say about his skating is that he never falls down. He's got very good balance.

Probably developed this good balance by carrying all that hair around on his head for so long.

I take Connie Pan by the hand. We just glide easy along. We're good skaters together.

In front of us, our E.S.L. party is struggling, but keeping together. The good skaters are buzzing in and out, going out in front of Beef, then skating back, coming close to him, dodging around him.

Beef's style is getting worse. He's bent over a bit. Tiring.

We're with thousands of people but we're starting to stand out.

His plan was probably to get lost in the crowd, get to the other end, ditch the skates, slip on the boots, jump in a cab, head for the airport with his money.

All along the sides of the world's longest skating rink the people are laughing and singing and swaying. They're happy because they're with their friends and it's winter and it's so beautiful out tonight. The lights along the ice make it hard to see the stars in the sky, but if you cup your mitts beside your eyes, if you shade your eyes from the lights and then lean your head back, you can see the stars, some of them, and you can catch the moon, the hooked moon, looking cozy up there in the frozen sky, following along with you, cruising along, keeping part of an eye on you.

If Beefaroni looks up he'll see the same stuff.

But he can't.

He's got other things on his mind.

And so have I.

The laneway man!

I call Detective Kennedy again.

We're approaching Pretoria Bridge.

There are cops on the bridge. I can see Kennedy up there, talking to me on the phone. I tell her about the laneway man and give her the address. She says she'll send a car over to his house.

"He's in there somewhere," I say.

She waves at me from the bridge.

"We'll pick Beefaroni up at the Arts Center," she says.

"If he makes it!" I say. "He's starting to come apart!"

There's more than just the E.S.L. skaters following

the "Follow me!" sign now. Looks like a lot of other people want to be in the E.S.L. party.

By the time we get to Pretoria Bridge there are thousands of Winterluders along the banks of the canal. The gang behind Beefaroni is getting bigger.

And the Beef's skating style is getting worse.

He's bent over farther and moving his arms in jerky motions. The boots around his neck are bothering him and his ankles are starting to bend.

Now we're at the wide turn and the straight stretch where you can see the Chateau Laurier and the Arts Center and the old train station and the Peace Tower. The way it looks, it looks like a picture of Russia or Mongolia or somewhere. Somewhere where it's beautiful. And where the buildings are shaped like ice and snow.

Beefaroni is now alone.

There's a crowd of more than a thousand people following him.

I phone ahead to Dink the Thinker to get him to order the beavertails.

I explain the situation.

"It's crawling with cops around here," says Dink. He's finding it hard to understand all at once.

"Just order the beavertails," I say. "I'll explain it all

later! Order an extra tail. Beefaroni's with us!" Before Dink can answer, I say, "Kirk out!"

Now, Beefaroni is the star of the show! Everybody's cheering him on!

He's not skating in a straight line anymore. He's wearing down. He's bent over and starting to look like a wind-up toy that needs to be wound up again.

Now his big fur hat is on the ice and a monster roar goes up!

Beefaroni is bald! He shaved his head!

Nobody but Connie Pan and me know who he is. Everybody thinks this is a clown act, part of Winterlude, and they give him a big cheer while he tries to get his hat back on.

There's quite a bit of steam coming off his head.

I'm starting to feel a little sorry for him.

He looks like he's finished. He looks like he's not going any farther.

He's standing there, looking down at his hat in his hands.

He's so weak he can hardly lift it.

But wait!

He's got a burst of adrenalin from somewhere.

He's going to take off! A last dash for freedom.

He's skating like a madman!

His legs are pumping and his head is back and his arms are flailing and he's sucking air.

Trouble is, he's not moving!

He's skating like a madman but he's not going anywhere!

He's like an exhausted athlete running on the spot.

But he's *skating* on the spot!

Everybody loves it.

It's the best clown act yet!

But it doesn't last. Now he's finished for sure.

The crowd goes "ahhh!" and gives Mr. B. Faroni a big hand. They like him.

Connie and me, we skate up and take Beef's arms. Some of the E.S.L. skaters crowd around to help. They've had a great time.

"Come on, Mr. Faroni," says Connie Pan. "Lean on us. We'll soon arrive. Where's all your nice beautiful hair gone?"

My phone rings.

It's Detective Kennedy.

They found the laneway man. He's OK.

He was tied with a rope in his kitchen where he could reach the sink and the fridge. Beef didn't want to hurt him. Just keep him quiet till he got out of Ottawa.

"An odd person, though," Kennedy adds. "Soon as

my cop untied him, he grabbed a shovel and went out and started shoveling his laneway!"

I can see Detective Kennedy talking to me on her phone at the end of the world's longest skating rink in a crowd of cops and Winterluders and photographers.

As we glide in, holding up Beefaroni, the cameras start flashing.

There's Dink the Thinker.

Time for a big snack of beavertails!

That's it, that's all!